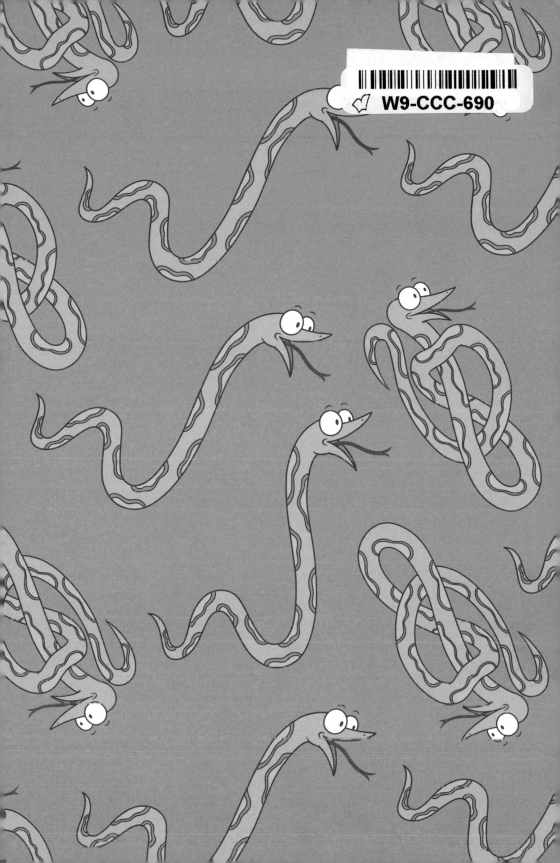

nickelodeon™

SANJAY & CRAIG™

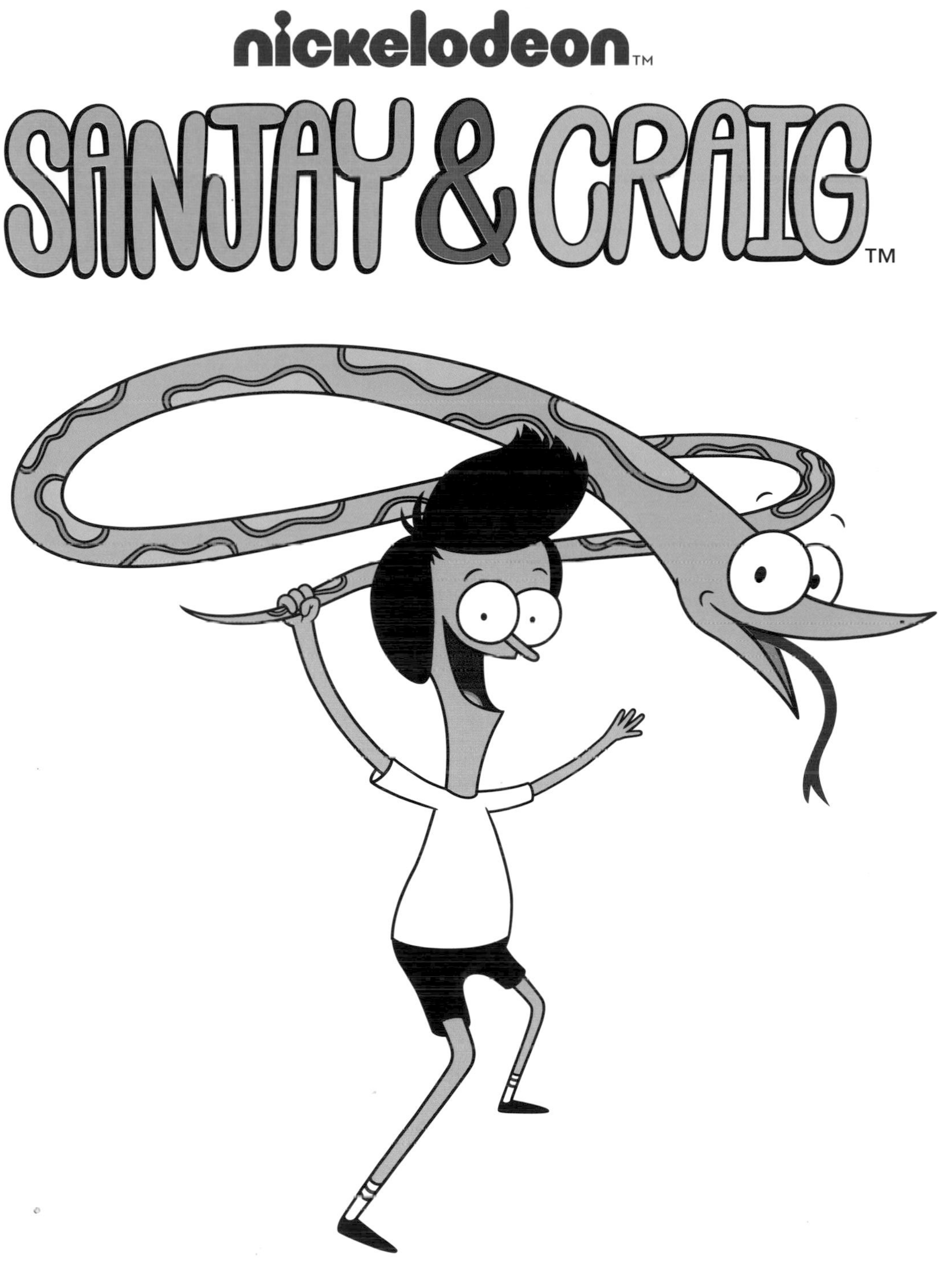

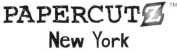

PAPERCUTZ™
New York

DUDE!

nickelodeon™
SANJAY AND CRAIG™

TABLE OF CONTENTS

SANJAY AND CRAIG™

#3 "STORY TIME WITH SANJAY AND CRAIG"

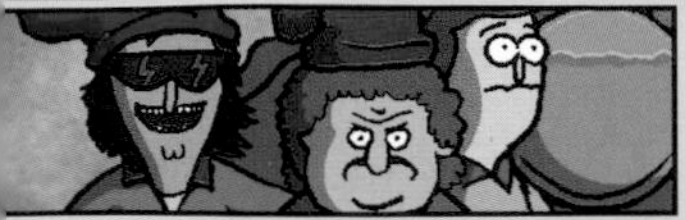

"STORY TIME WITH SANJAY AND CRAIG"
Eric Esquivel – Writer
Cliff Galbraith – Artist & Letterer
Laurie E. Smith – Colorist

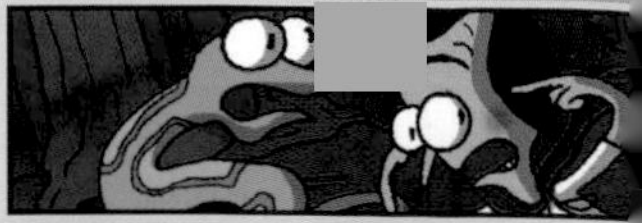

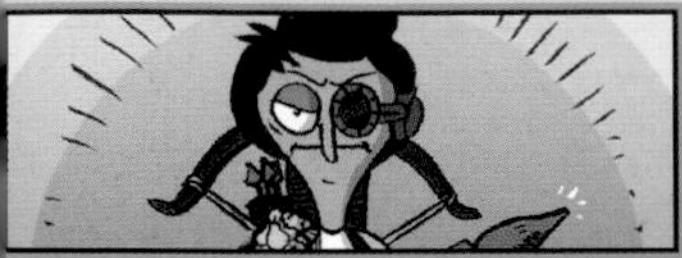

"NEW KID ON THE BLOCK"
Eric Esquivel – Writer
James Kaminski – Artist
Laurie E. Smith – Colorist
Tom Orzechowski – Letterer

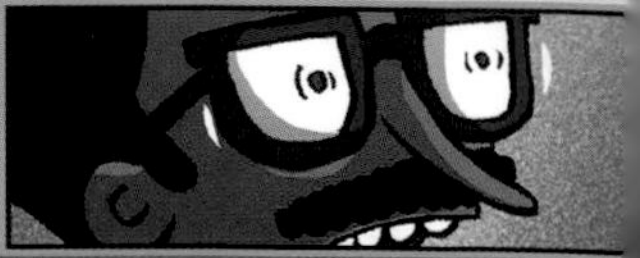

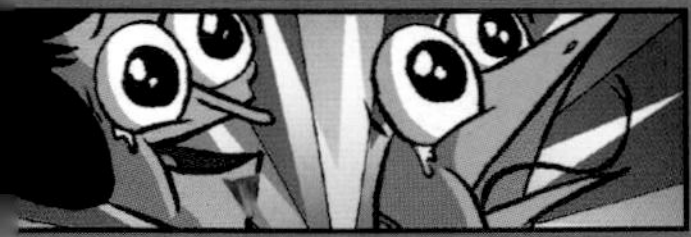

"YOU FEELIN' LUCKY, PUNK?"
Eric Esquivel – Writer
James Kaminski – Artist
Laurie E. Smith – Colorist
Tom Orzechowski – Letterer

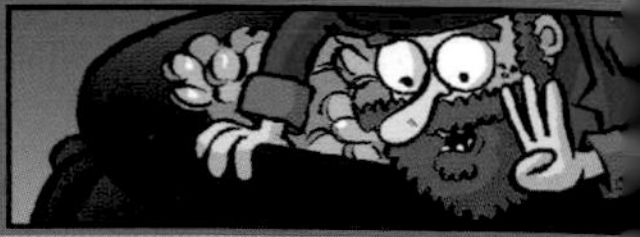

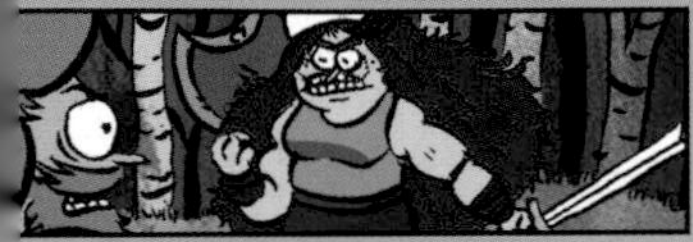

"SEASON 12, EPISODE ONE BILLION"
Eric Esquivel – Writer
James Kaminski – Artist
Matt Herms – Colorist
Tom Orzechowski – Letterer

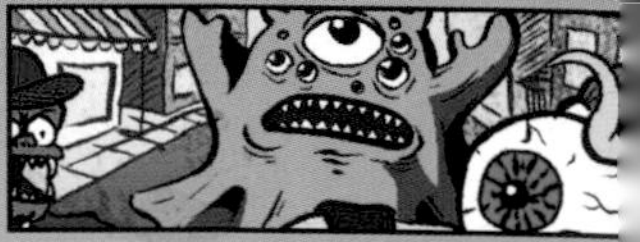

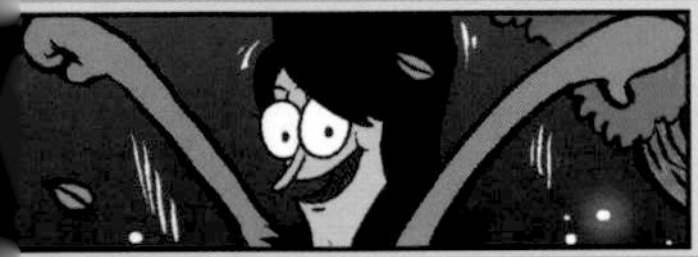

"THE HUGGLE IS REAL"
Eric Esquivel – Writer
James Kaminski – Artist
Matt Herms – Colorist
Tom Orzechowski – Letterer

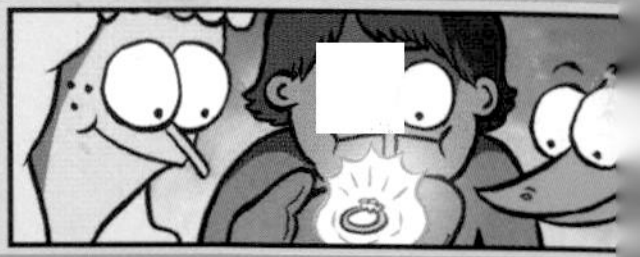

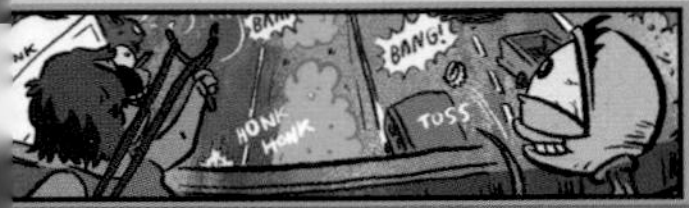
BANG!
HONK HONK
TOSS

"HECTOR AND SEÑOR OJO"
Eric Esquivel – Writer
Sam Spina – Artist & Letterer
Matt Herms – Colorist

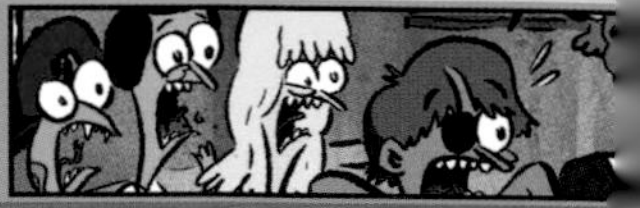

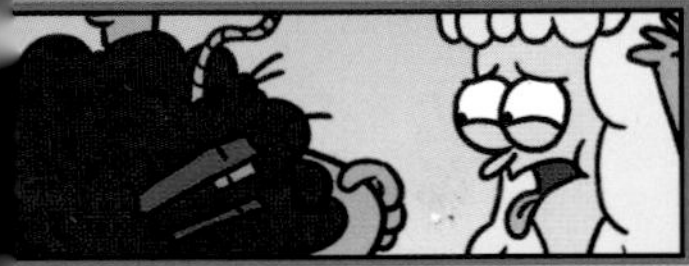

"WING NUTS" by Josh Engel
"NAH, DAWG" by Aminder Dhaliwal
"HAPPY PLACE" by Gina Gress
"COOKING WITH TUFFLIPS" by Josh Engel
"SANJAY AND CRAIG!" by Mike Bertino

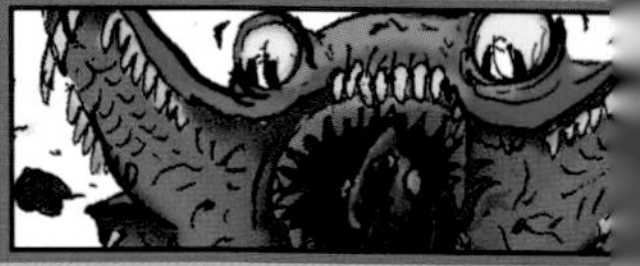

Based on the Nickelodeon animated TV series created by Jim Dirschberger, Andreas Trolf, and Jay Howell.

James Salerno – Sr. Art Director/Nickelodeon
Chris Nelson – Design/Production
Jeff Whitman – Production Coordinator
Bethany Bryan – Editor
Joan Hilty – Comics Editor/Nickelodeon
Isabella van Ingen – Editorial Intern
Jim Salicrup
Editor-in-Chief

ISBN: 978-1-62991-464-0 paperback edition
ISBN: 978-1-62991-463-3 hardcover edition

Papercutz books may be purchased for business or promotional use. For information on bulk purchases please contact Macmillan Corporate and Premium Sales Department at (800) 221-7945 x5442.

Printed in Korea
May 2016 by
We SP Co., LTD.
79-29, Sotaji-ro,
Paju-Si, Gyeonggi-do, 10863
Seoul, Gyeonggi-do 413-756

Distributed by Macmillan

First Printing

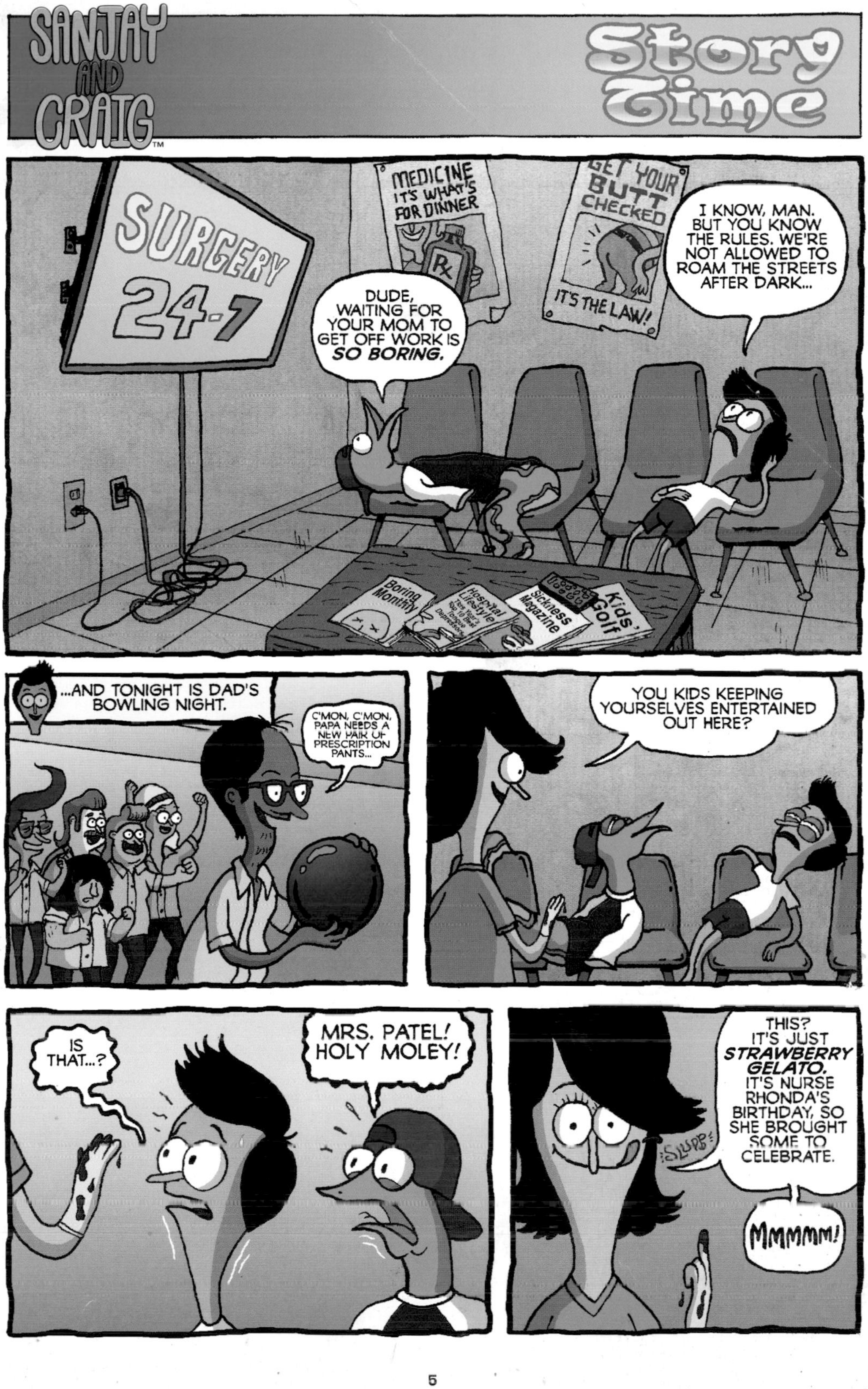

SANJAY AND CRAIG™
Story Time
SURGERY 24-7
MEDICINE IT'S WHAT'S FOR DINNER
GET YOUR BUTT CHECKED
IT'S THE LAW!
DUDE, WAITING FOR YOUR MOM TO GET OFF WORK IS *SO BORING.*
I KNOW, MAN. BUT YOU KNOW THE RULES. WE'RE NOT ALLOWED TO ROAM THE STREETS AFTER DARK...
Boring Monthly
Hospital Lifestyle
Sickness Magazine
Kids' Golf
...AND TONIGHT IS DAD'S BOWLING NIGHT.
C'MON, C'MON, PAPA NEEDS A NEW PAIR OF PRESCRIPTION PANTS...
YOU KIDS KEEPING YOURSELVES ENTERTAINED OUT HERE?
IS THAT...?
MRS. PATEL! HOLY MOLEY!
SLURP
THIS? IT'S JUST *STRAWBERRY GELATO.* IT'S NURSE RHONDA'S BIRTHDAY, SO SHE BROUGHT SOME TO CELEBRATE.
MMMMM!

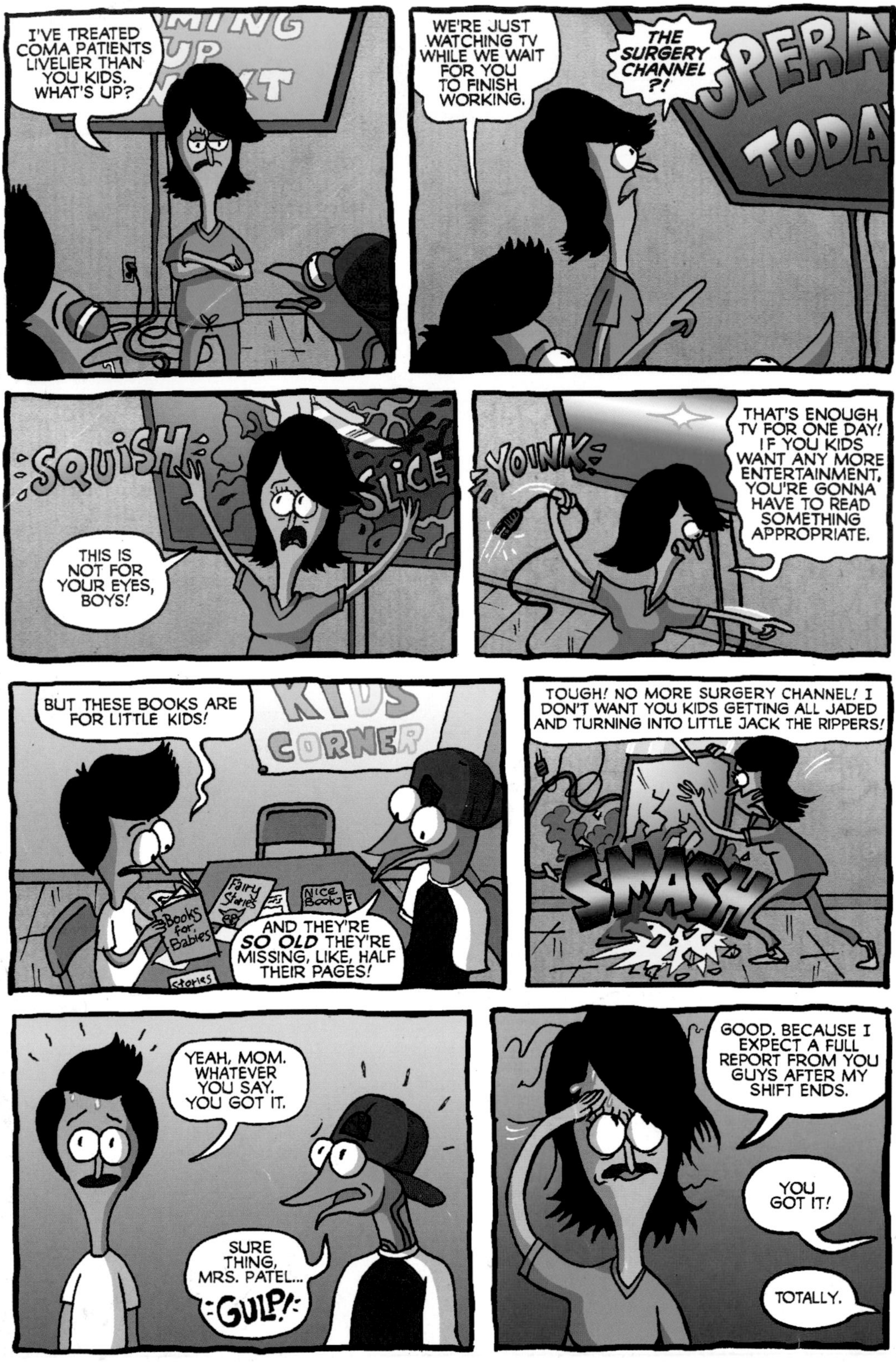
I'VE TREATED COMA PATIENTS LIVELIER THAN YOU KIDS. WHAT'S UP?
WE'RE JUST WATCHING TV WHILE WE WAIT FOR YOU TO FINISH WORKING.
THE SURGERY CHANNEL ?!
SQUISH
SLICE
THIS IS NOT FOR YOUR EYES, BOYS!
YOINK
THAT'S ENOUGH TV FOR ONE DAY! IF YOU KIDS WANT ANY MORE ENTERTAINMENT, YOU'RE GONNA HAVE TO READ SOMETHING APPROPRIATE.
BUT THESE BOOKS ARE FOR LITTLE KIDS!
KIDS CORNER
Books for Babies
Fairy Stories
NICE Books
Stories
AND THEY'RE SO OLD THEY'RE MISSING, LIKE, HALF THEIR PAGES!
TOUGH! NO MORE SURGERY CHANNEL! I DON'T WANT YOU KIDS GETTING ALL JADED AND TURNING INTO LITTLE JACK THE RIPPERS!
SMASH
YEAH, MOM. WHATEVER YOU SAY. YOU GOT IT.
SURE THING, MRS. PATEL...
GULP!
GOOD. BECAUSE I EXPECT A FULL REPORT FROM YOU GUYS AFTER MY SHIFT ENDS.
YOU GOT IT!
TOTALLY.

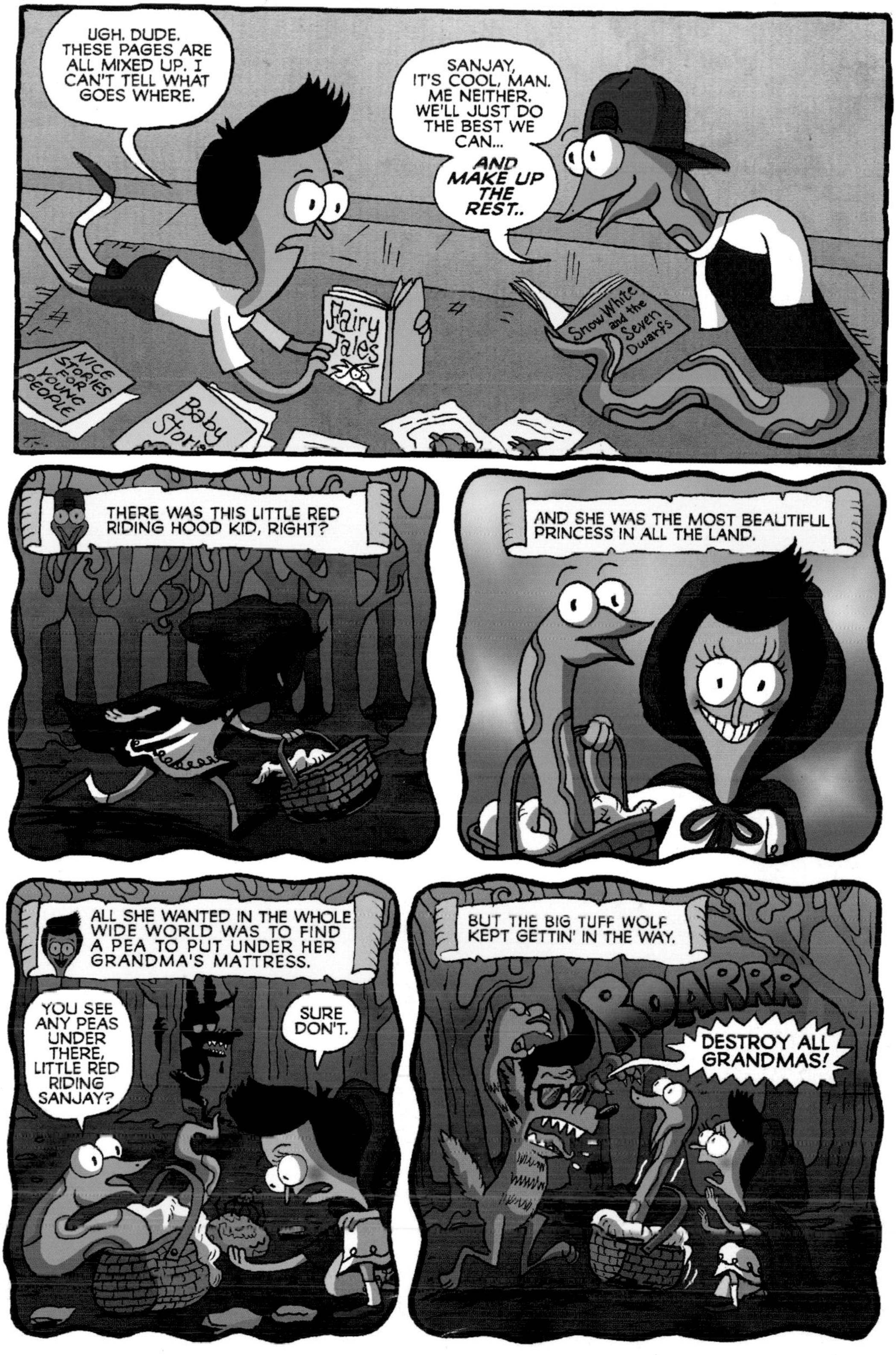

UGH. DUDE. THESE PAGES ARE ALL MIXED UP. I CAN'T TELL WHAT GOES WHERE.
SANJAY, IT'S COOL, MAN. ME NEITHER. WE'LL JUST DO THE BEST WE CAN...
AND MAKE UP THE REST..
Fairy Tales
Snow White and the Seven Dwarfs
NICE STORIES FOR YOUNG PEOPLE
Baby Stories
THERE WAS THIS LITTLE RED RIDING HOOD KID, RIGHT?
AND SHE WAS THE MOST BEAUTIFUL PRINCESS IN ALL THE LAND.
ALL SHE WANTED IN THE WHOLE WIDE WORLD WAS TO FIND A PEA TO PUT UNDER HER GRANDMA'S MATTRESS.
YOU SEE ANY PEAS UNDER THERE, LITTLE RED RIDING SANJAY?
SURE DON'T.
BUT THE BIG TUFF WOLF KEPT GETTIN' IN THE WAY.
ROARRR
DESTROY ALL GRANDMAS!

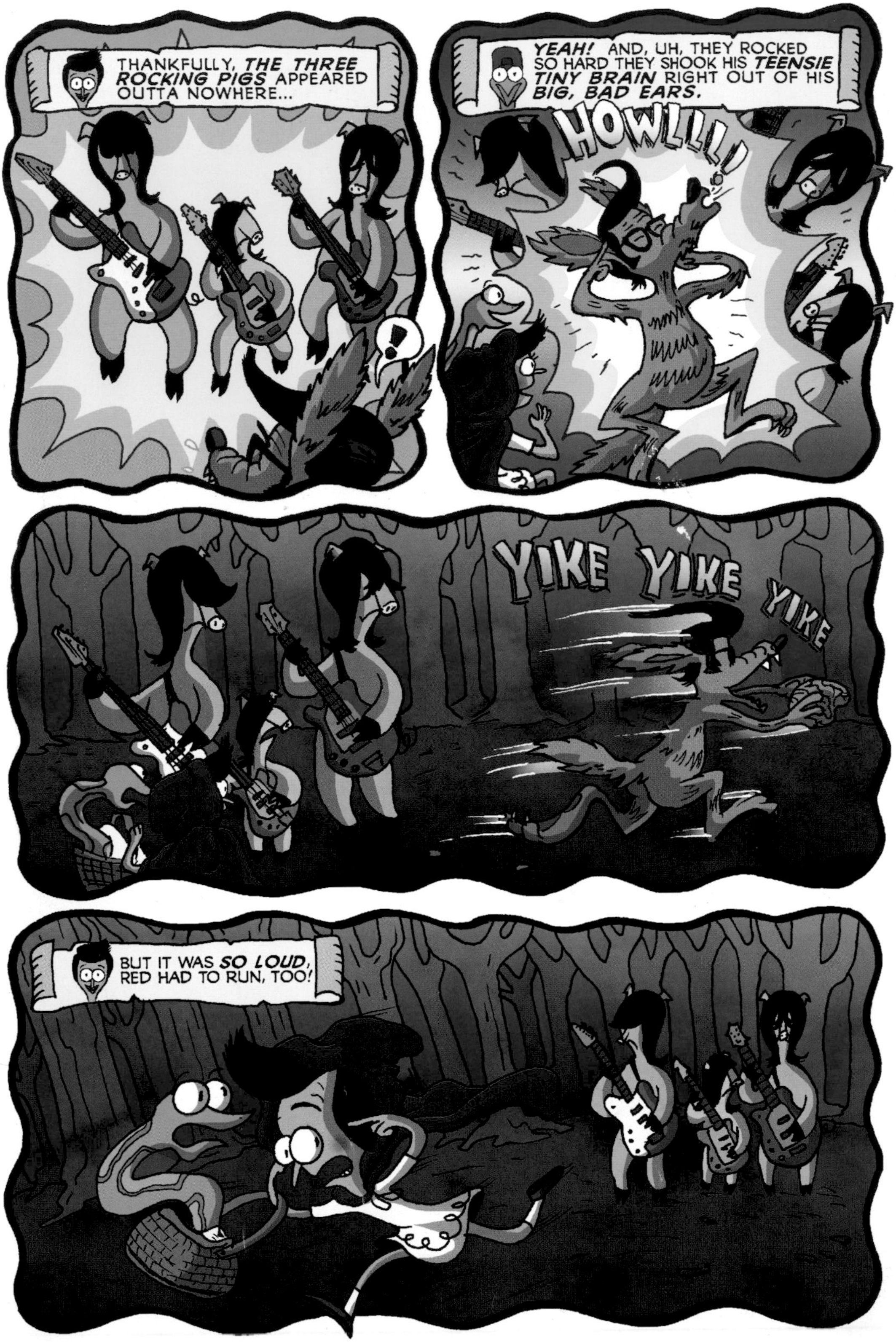
THANKFULLY, THE THREE ROCKING PIGS APPEARED OUTTA NOWHERE...
!
YEAH! AND, UH, THEY ROCKED SO HARD THEY SHOOK HIS TEENSIE TINY BRAIN RIGHT OUT OF HIS BIG, BAD EARS.
HOWLLL!
YIKE YIKE YIKE
BUT IT WAS SO LOUD, RED HAD TO RUN, TOO!

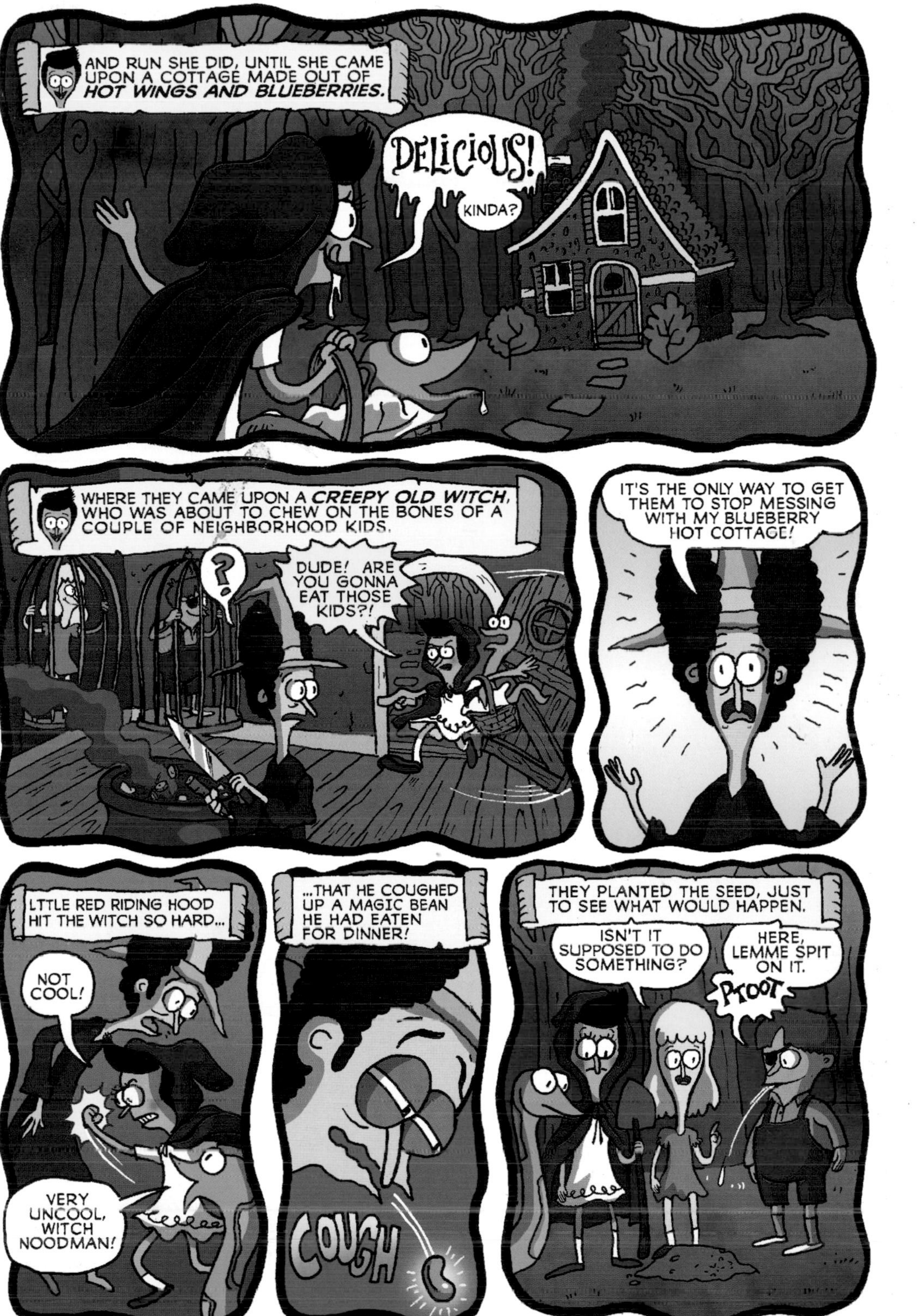
AND RUN SHE DID, UNTIL SHE CAME UPON A COTTAGE MADE OUT OF ***HOT WINGS AND BLUEBERRIES.***
DELICIOUS!
KINDA?
WHERE THEY CAME UPON A ***CREEPY OLD WITCH,*** WHO WAS ABOUT TO CHEW ON THE BONES OF A COUPLE OF NEIGHBORHOOD KIDS.
?
DUDE! ARE YOU GONNA EAT THOSE KIDS?!
IT'S THE ONLY WAY TO GET THEM TO STOP MESSING WITH MY BLUEBERRY HOT COTTAGE!
LTTLE RED RIDING HOOD HIT THE WITCH SO HARD...
NOT COOL!
VERY UNCOOL, WITCH NOODMAN!
...THAT HE COUGHED UP A MAGIC BEAN HE HAD EATEN FOR DINNER!
COUGH
THEY PLANTED THE SEED, JUST TO SEE WHAT WOULD HAPPEN.
ISN'T IT SUPPOSED TO DO SOMETHING?
HERE, LEMME SPIT ON IT.
PTOOT

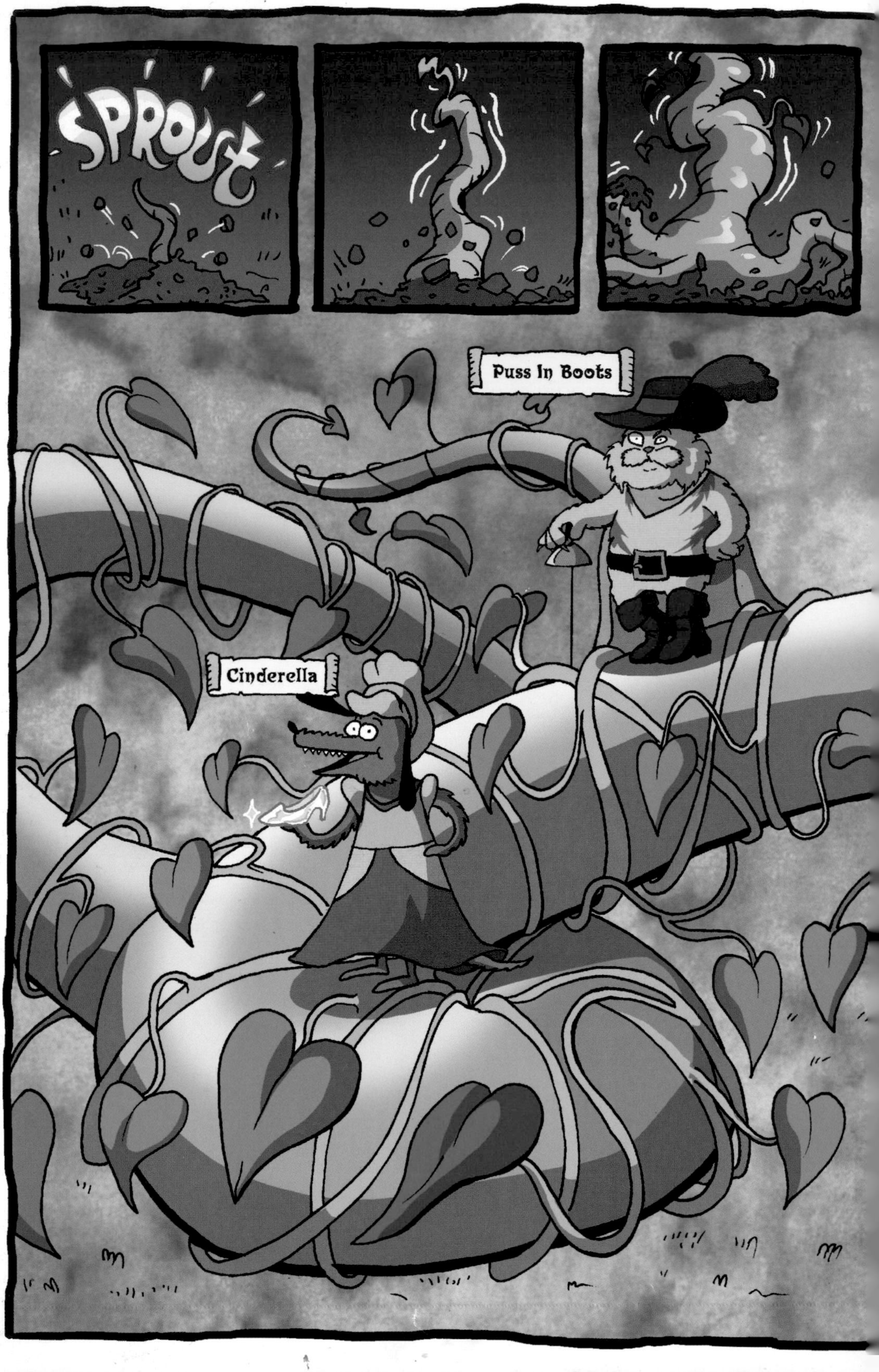
SPROUT
Puss In Boots
Cinderella

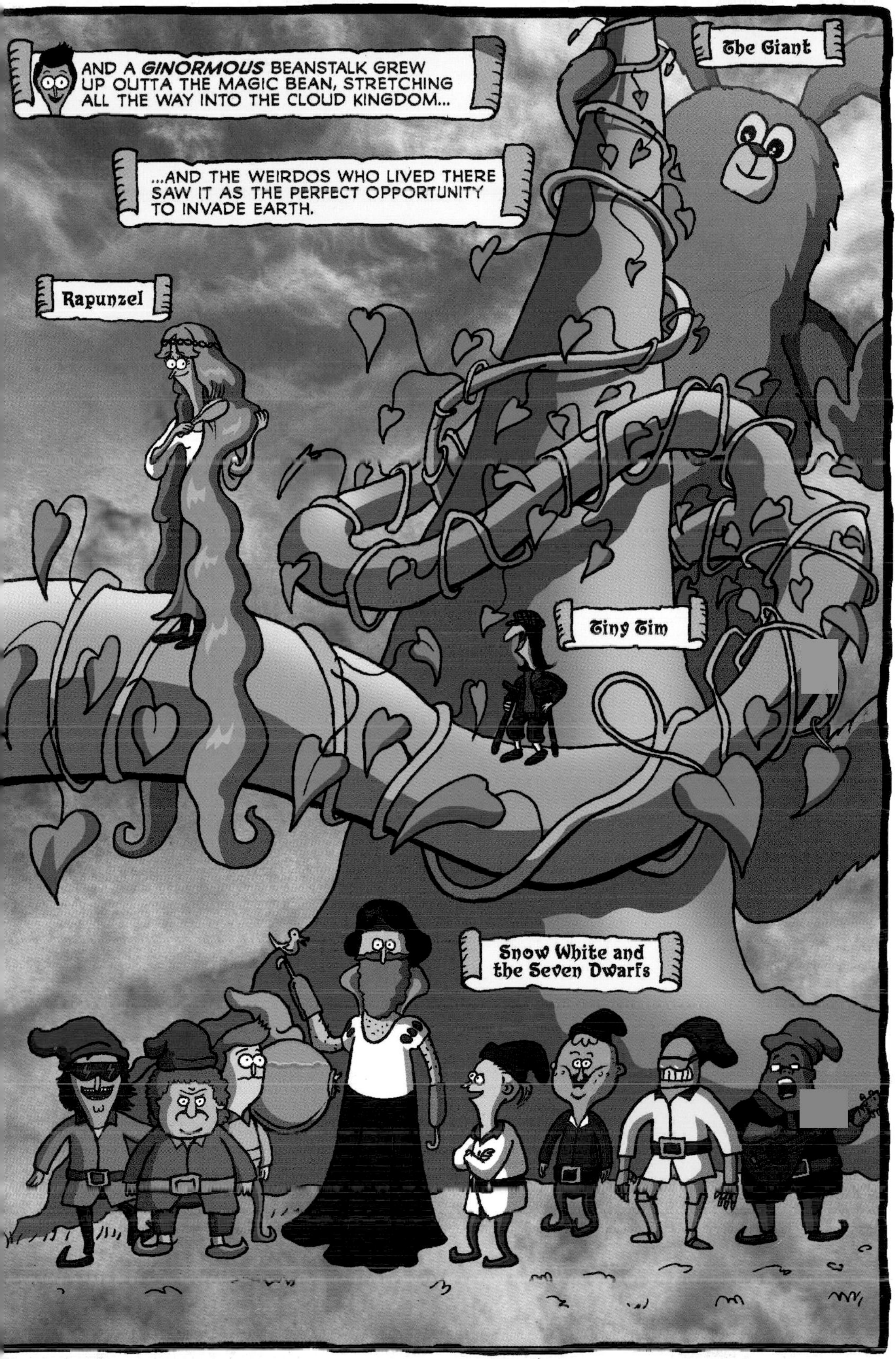
AND A GINORMOUS BEANSTALK GREW UP OUTTA THE MAGIC BEAN, STRETCHING ALL THE WAY INTO THE CLOUD KINGDOM...
...AND THE WEIRDOS WHO LIVED THERE SAW IT AS THE PERFECT OPPORTUNITY TO INVADE EARTH.
The Giant
Rapunzel
Tiny Tim
Snow White and the Seven Dwarfs

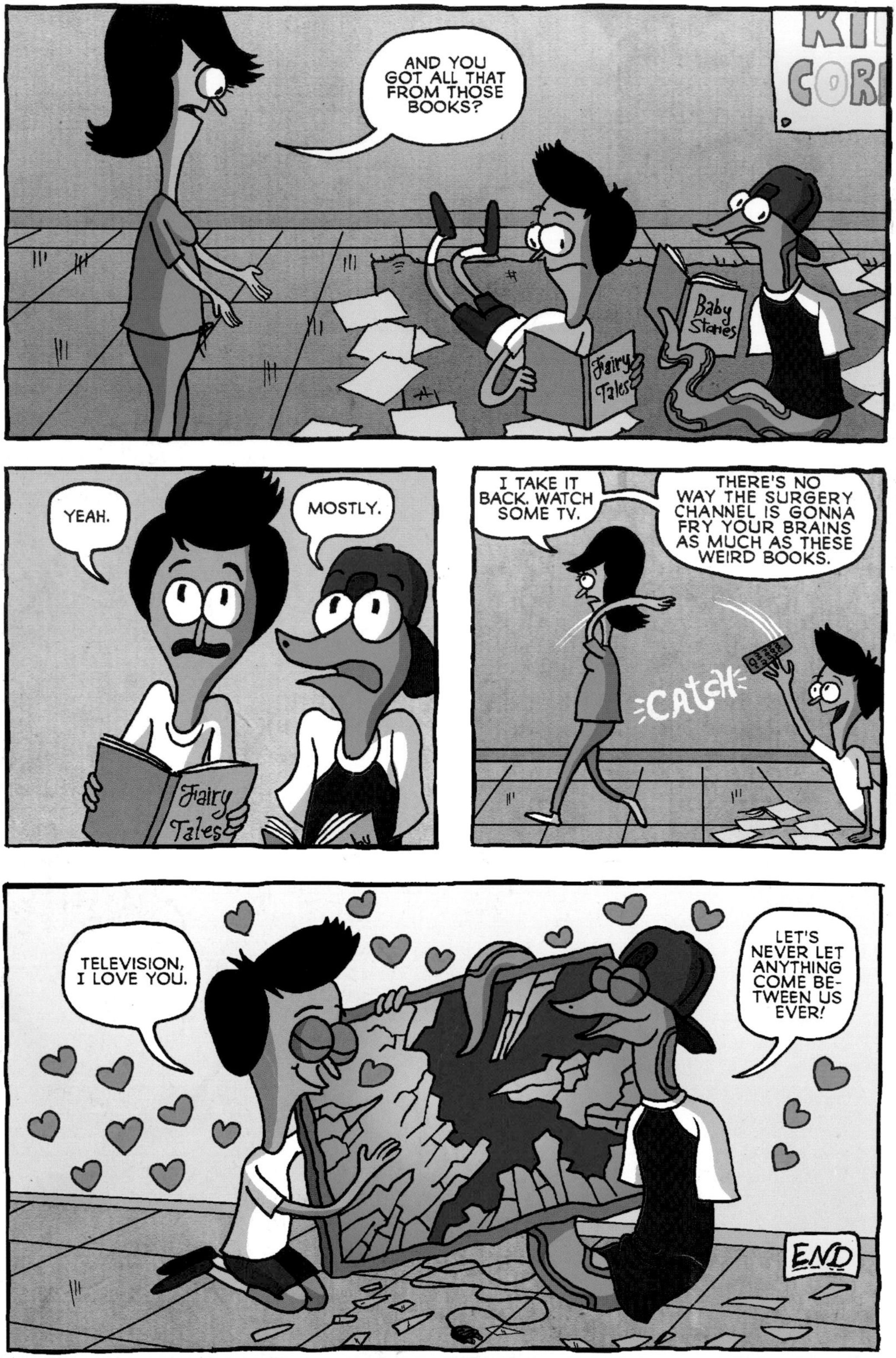
AND YOU GOT ALL THAT FROM THOSE BOOKS?
Fairy Tales
Baby Stories
YEAH.
MOSTLY.
Fairy Tales
I TAKE IT BACK. WATCH SOME TV.
THERE'S NO WAY THE SURGERY CHANNEL IS GONNA FRY YOUR BRAINS AS MUCH AS THESE WEIRD BOOKS.
CATCH
TELEVISION, I LOVE YOU.
LET'S NEVER LET ANYTHING COME BE- TWEEN US EVER!
END

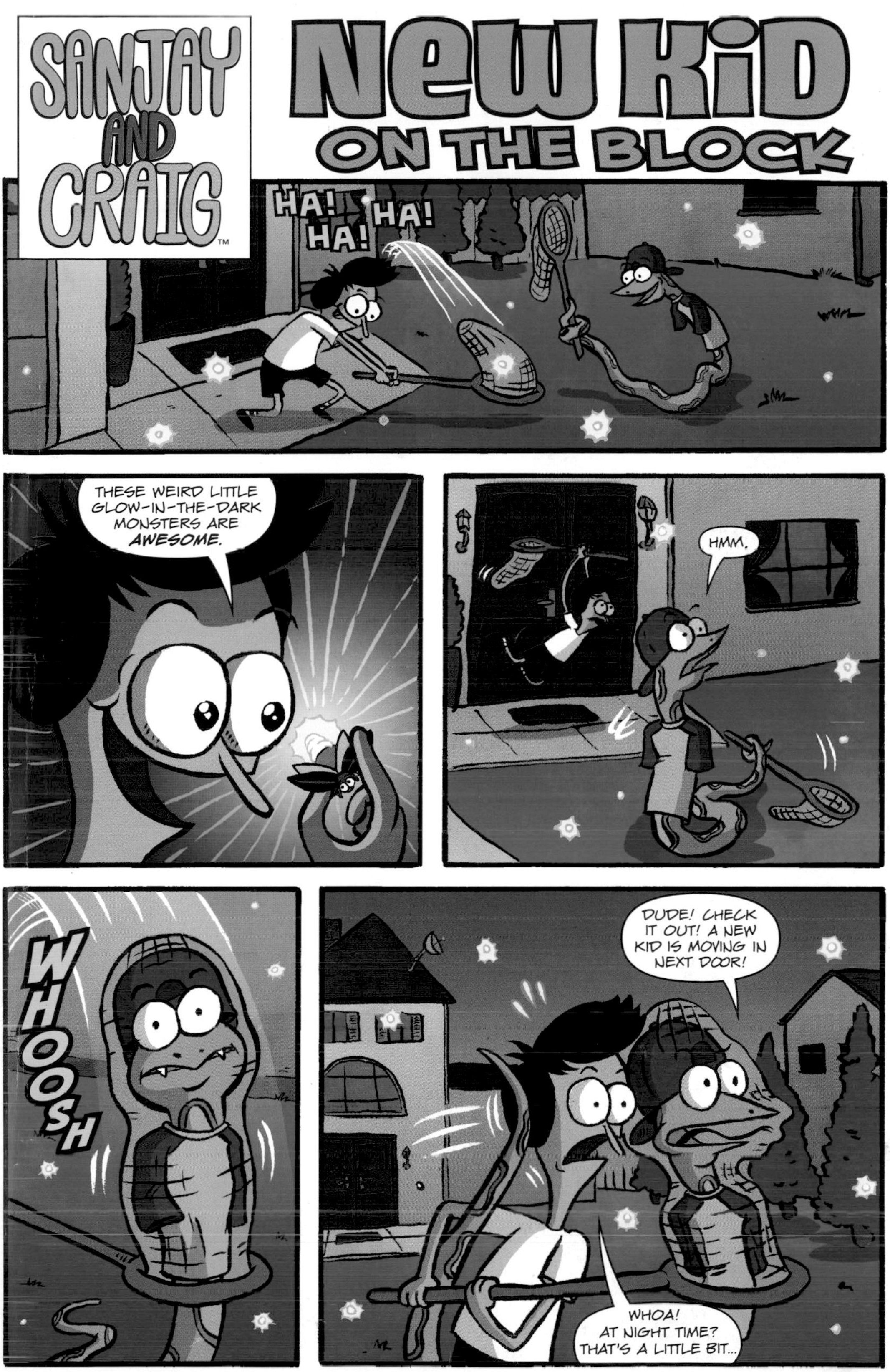

SANJAY AND CRAIG™
NEW KID ON THE BLOCK
HA! HA! HA!
THESE WEIRD LITTLE GLOW-IN-THE-DARK MONSTERS ARE AWESOME.
HMM.
WHOOSH
DUDE! CHECK IT OUT! A NEW KID IS MOVING IN NEXT DOOR!
WHOA! AT NIGHT TIME? THAT'S A LITTLE BIT...

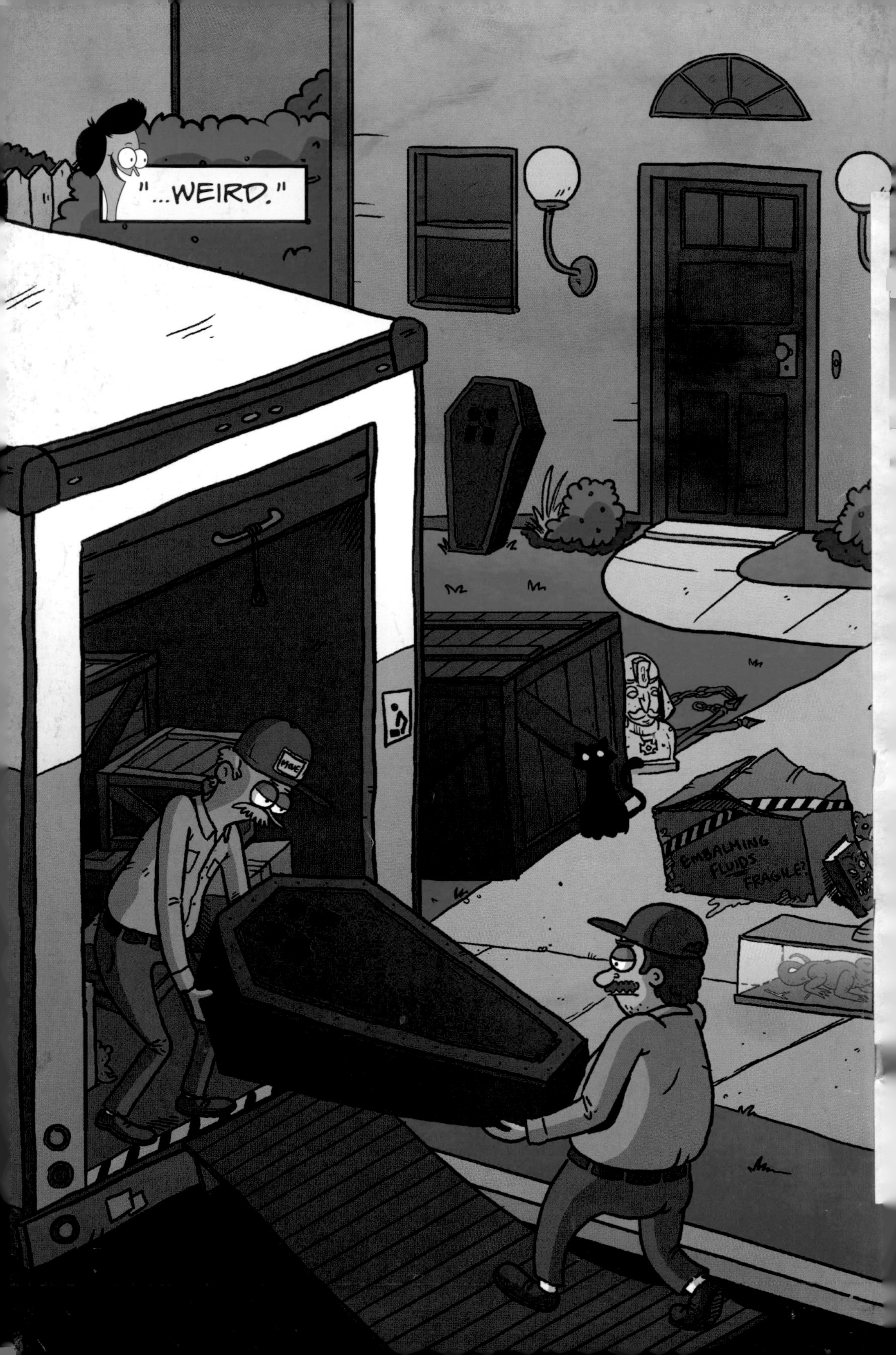
"...WEIRD."
EMBALMING FLUIDS FRAGILE?

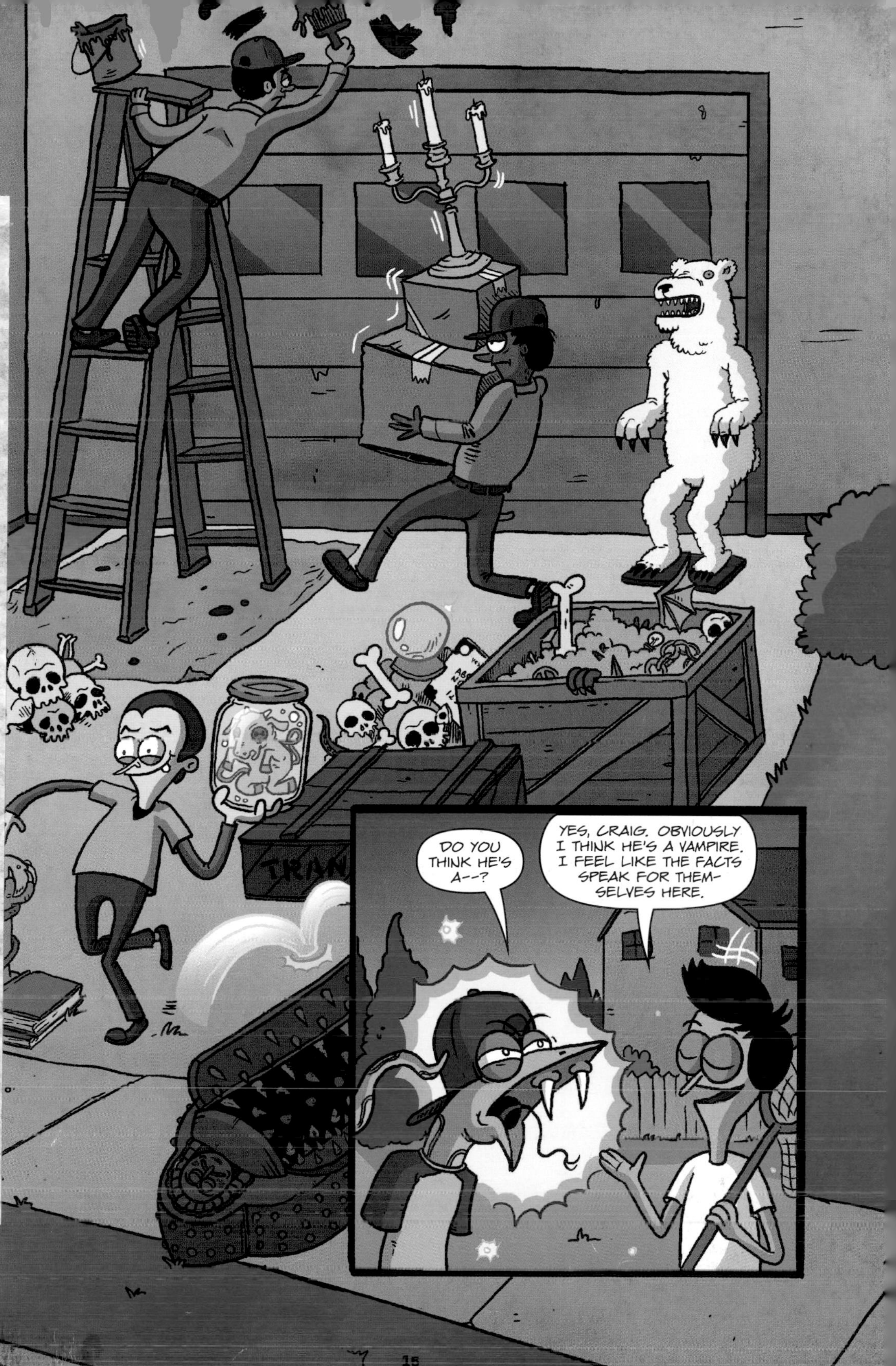
TRAN
DO YOU THINK HE'S A--?
YES, CRAIG. OBVIOUSLY I THINK HE'S A VAMPIRE. I FEEL LIKE THE FACTS SPEAK FOR THEMSELVES HERE.

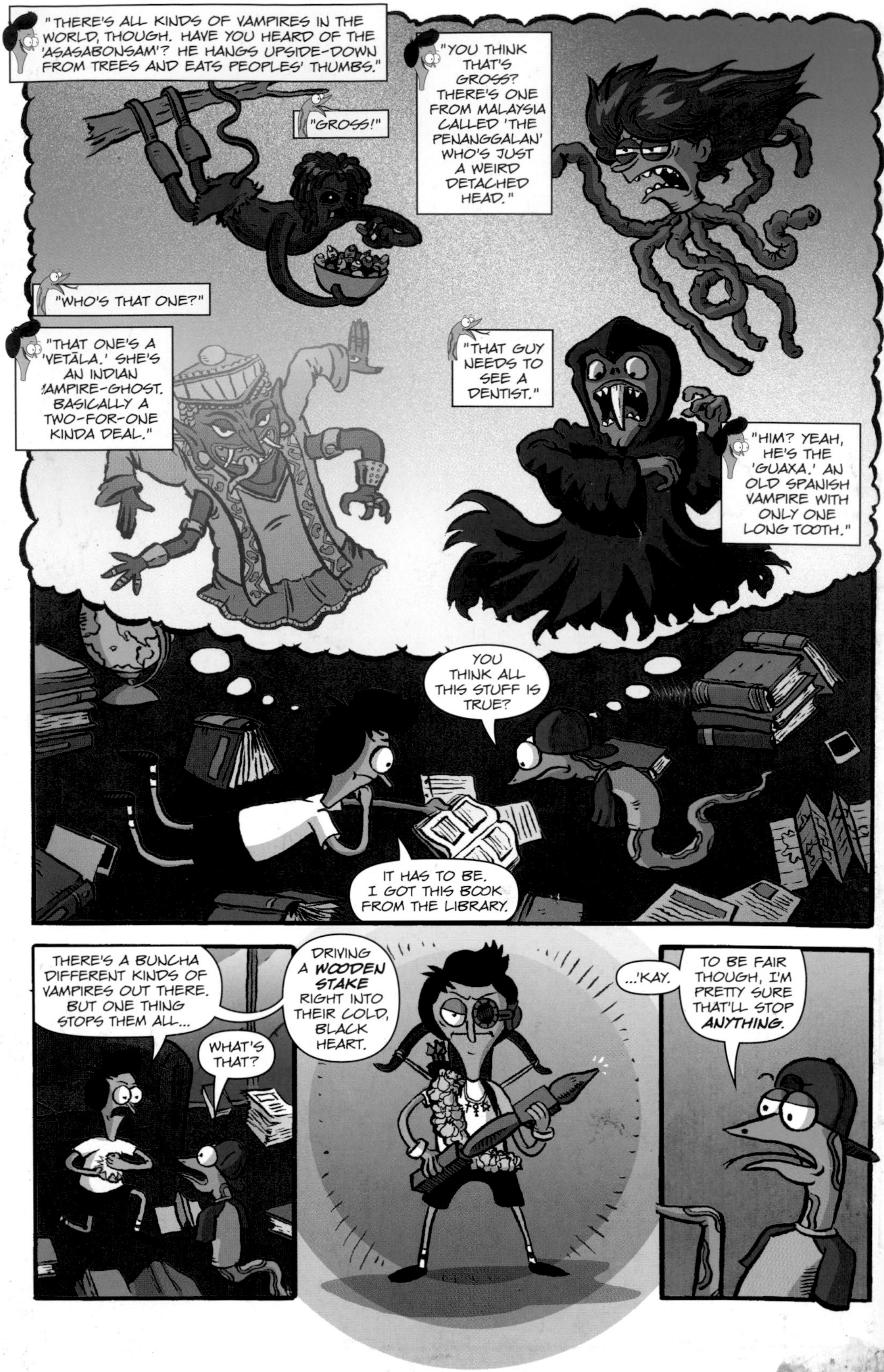
"THERE'S ALL KINDS OF VAMPIRES IN THE WORLD, THOUGH. HAVE YOU HEARD OF THE 'ASASABONSAM'? HE HANGS UPSIDE-DOWN FROM TREES AND EATS PEOPLES' THUMBS."
"GROSS!"
"YOU THINK THAT'S GROSS? THERE'S ONE FROM MALAYSIA CALLED 'THE PENANGGALAN' WHO'S JUST A WEIRD DETACHED HEAD."
"WHO'S THAT ONE?"
"THAT ONE'S A 'VETĀLA.' SHE'S AN INDIAN VAMPIRE-GHOST. BASICALLY A TWO-FOR-ONE KINDA DEAL."
"THAT GUY NEEDS TO SEE A DENTIST."
"HIM? YEAH, HE'S THE 'GUAXA.' AN OLD SPANISH VAMPIRE WITH ONLY ONE LONG TOOTH."
YOU THINK ALL THIS STUFF IS TRUE?
IT HAS TO BE. I GOT THIS BOOK FROM THE LIBRARY.
THERE'S A BUNCHA DIFFERENT KINDS OF VAMPIRES OUT THERE. BUT ONE THING STOPS THEM ALL...
WHAT'S THAT?
DRIVING A **WOODEN STAKE** RIGHT INTO THEIR COLD, BLACK HEART.
...'KAY.
TO BE FAIR THOUGH, I'M PRETTY SURE THAT'LL STOP **ANYTHING**.

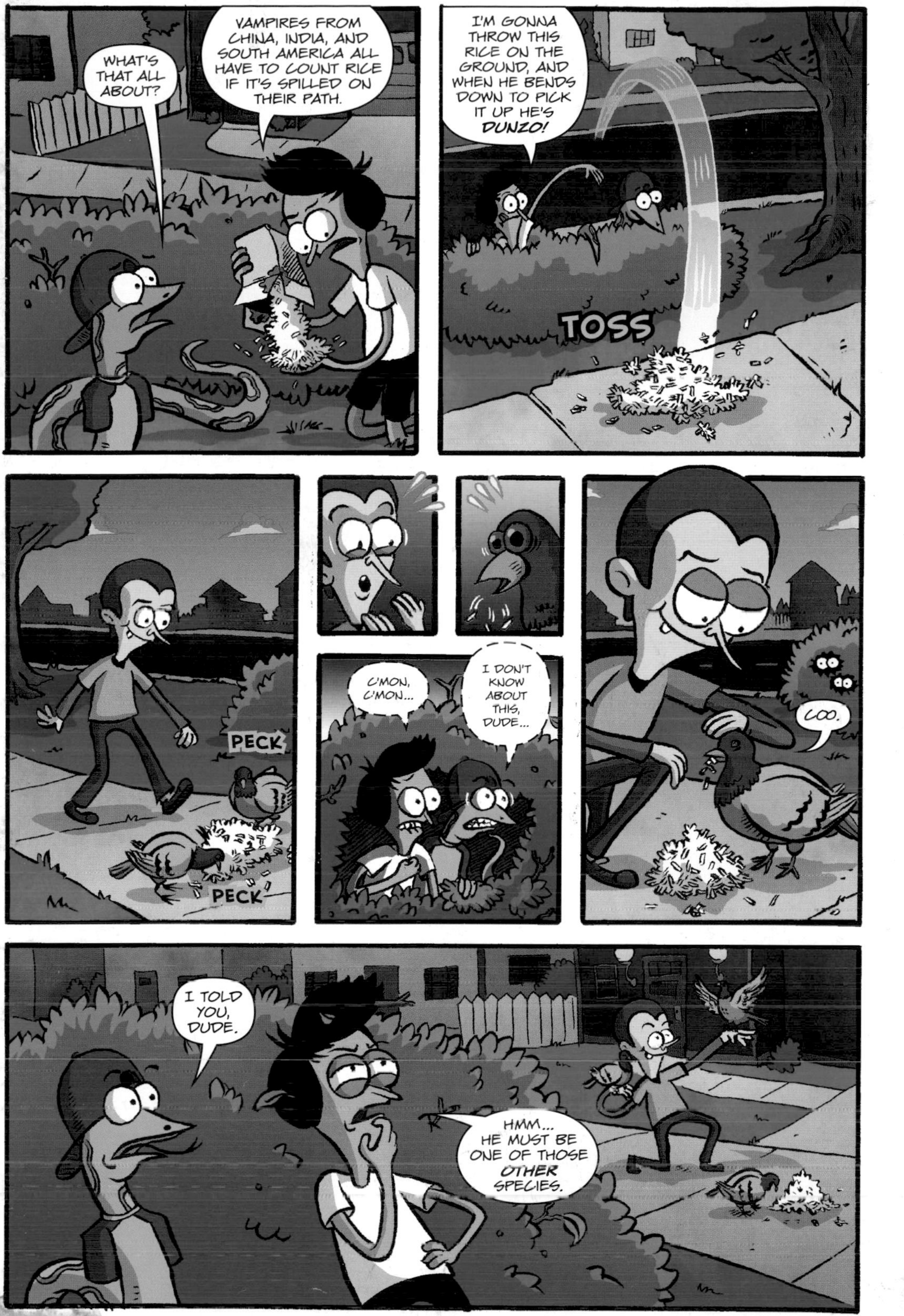
WHAT'S THAT ALL ABOUT?
VAMPIRES FROM CHINA, INDIA, AND SOUTH AMERICA ALL HAVE TO COUNT RICE IF IT'S SPILLED ON THEIR PATH.
I'M GONNA THROW THIS RICE ON THE GROUND, AND WHEN HE BENDS DOWN TO PICK IT UP HE'S *DUNZO!*
TOSS
PECK
PECK
C'MON, C'MON...
I DON'T KNOW ABOUT THIS, DUDE...
COO.
I TOLD YOU, DUDE.
HMM... HE MUST BE ONE OF THOSE *OTHER* SPECIES.

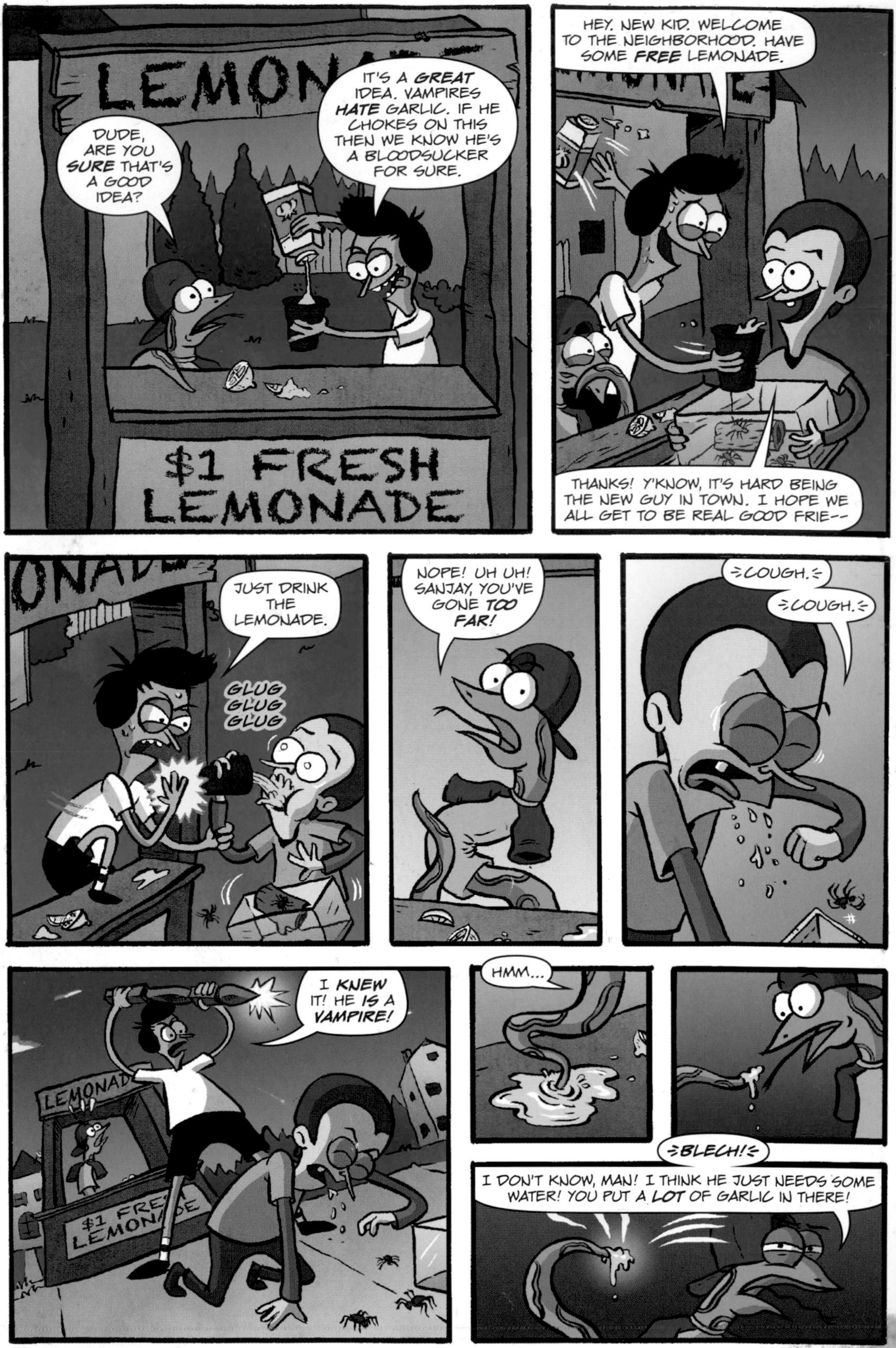
LEMON
DUDE, ARE YOU SURE THAT'S A GOOD IDEA?
IT'S A GREAT IDEA. VAMPIRES HATE GARLIC. IF HE CHOKES ON THIS THEN WE KNOW HE'S A BLOODSUCKER FOR SURE.
$1 FRESH LEMONADE
HEY. NEW KID. WELCOME TO THE NEIGHBORHOOD. HAVE SOME FREE LEMONADE.
THANKS! Y'KNOW, IT'S HARD BEING THE NEW GUY IN TOWN. I HOPE WE ALL GET TO BE REAL GOOD FRIE--
JUST DRINK THE LEMONADE.
GLUG GLUG GLUG
NOPE! UH UH! SANJAY, YOU'VE GONE TOO FAR!
COUGH.
COUGH.
I KNEW IT! HE IS A VAMPIRE!
LEMONADE
$1 FRESH LEMONADE
HMM...
BLECH!
I DON'T KNOW, MAN! I THINK HE JUST NEEDS SOME WATER! YOU PUT A LOT OF GARLIC IN THERE!

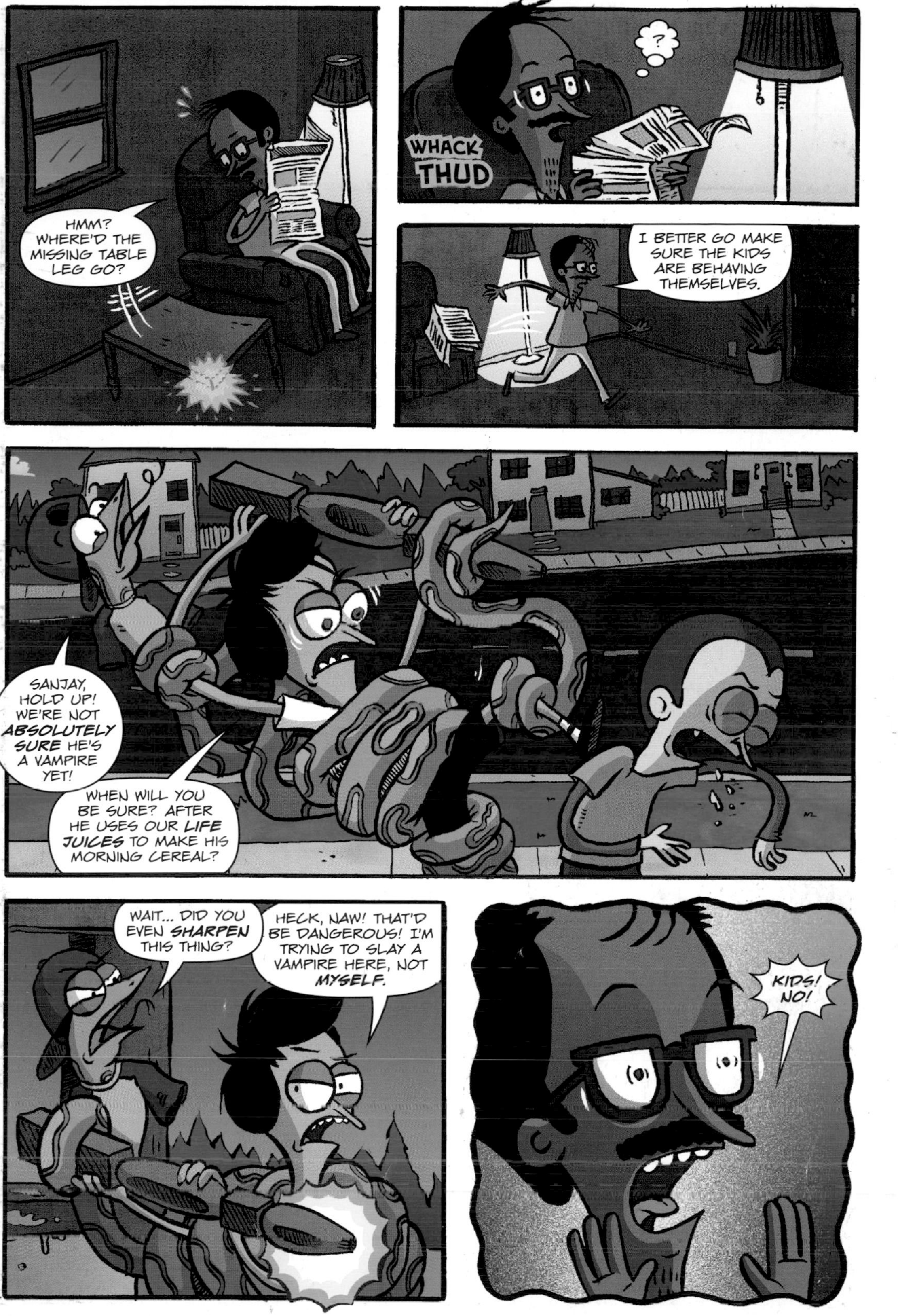
HMM? WHERE'D THE MISSING TABLE LEG GO?
WHACK
THUD
?
I BETTER GO MAKE SURE THE KIDS ARE BEHAVING THEMSELVES.
SANJAY, HOLD UP! WE'RE NOT ABSOLUTELY SURE HE'S A VAMPIRE YET!
WHEN WILL YOU BE SURE? AFTER HE USES OUR LIFE JUICES TO MAKE HIS MORNING CEREAL?
WAIT... DID YOU EVEN SHARPEN THIS THING?
HECK, NAW! THAT'D BE DANGEROUS! I'M TRYING TO SLAY A VAMPIRE HERE, NOT MYSELF.
KIDS! NO!

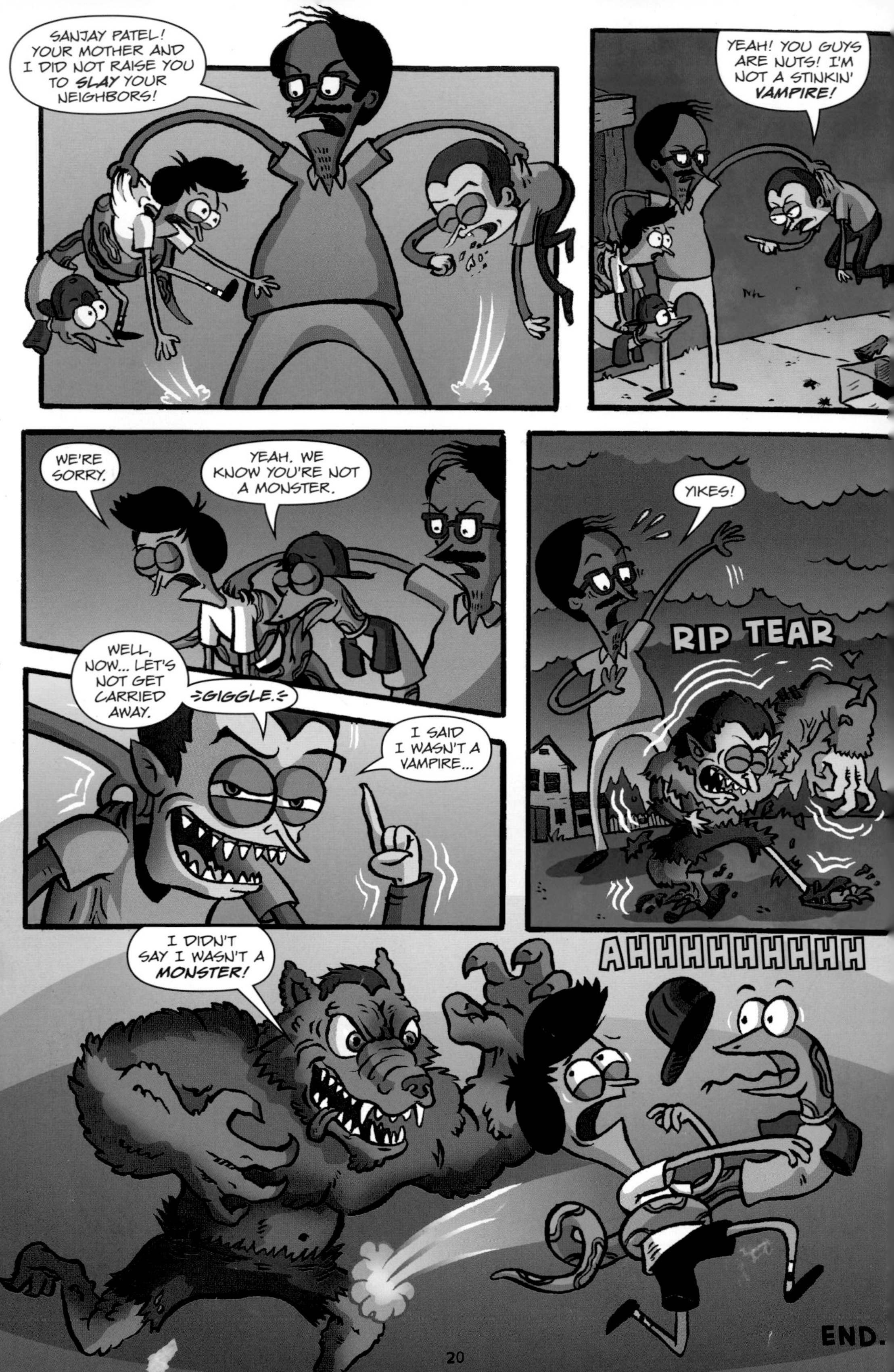
SANJAY PATEL! YOUR MOTHER AND I DID NOT RAISE YOU TO SLAY YOUR NEIGHBORS!
YEAH! YOU GUYS ARE NUTS! I'M NOT A STINKIN' VAMPIRE!
WE'RE SORRY.
YEAH. WE KNOW YOU'RE NOT A MONSTER.
WELL, NOW... LET'S NOT GET CARRIED AWAY.
GIGGLE.
I SAID I WASN'T A VAMPIRE...
YIKES!
RIP TEAR
I DIDN'T SAY I WASN'T A MONSTER!
AHHHHHHHHHH
END.

WING NUTS

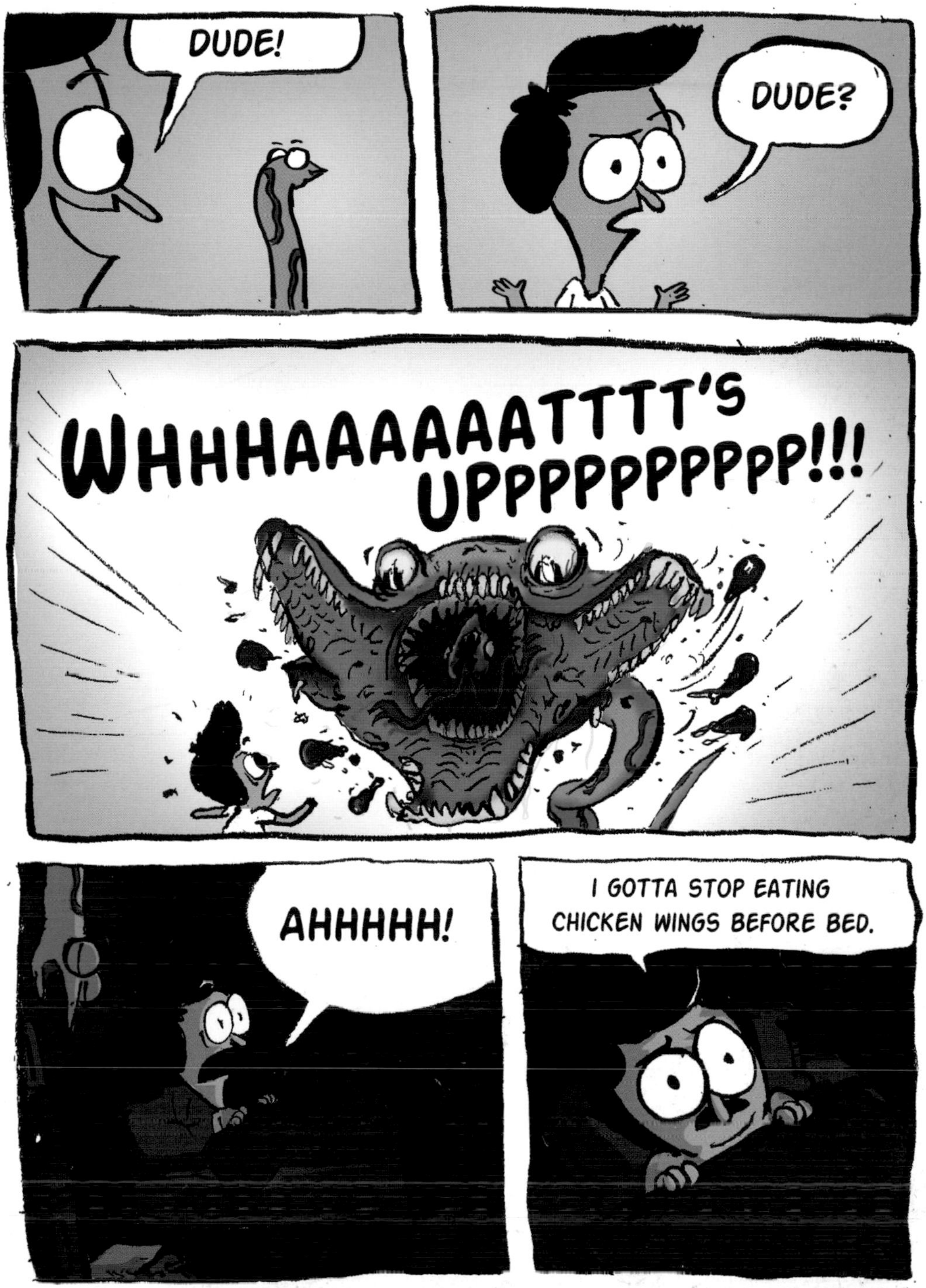

DUDE!
DUDE?
WHHHAAAAAAATTTT'S UPPPPPPPPPP!!!
AHHHHH!
I GOTTA STOP EATING CHICKEN WINGS BEFORE BED.

Josh Engel

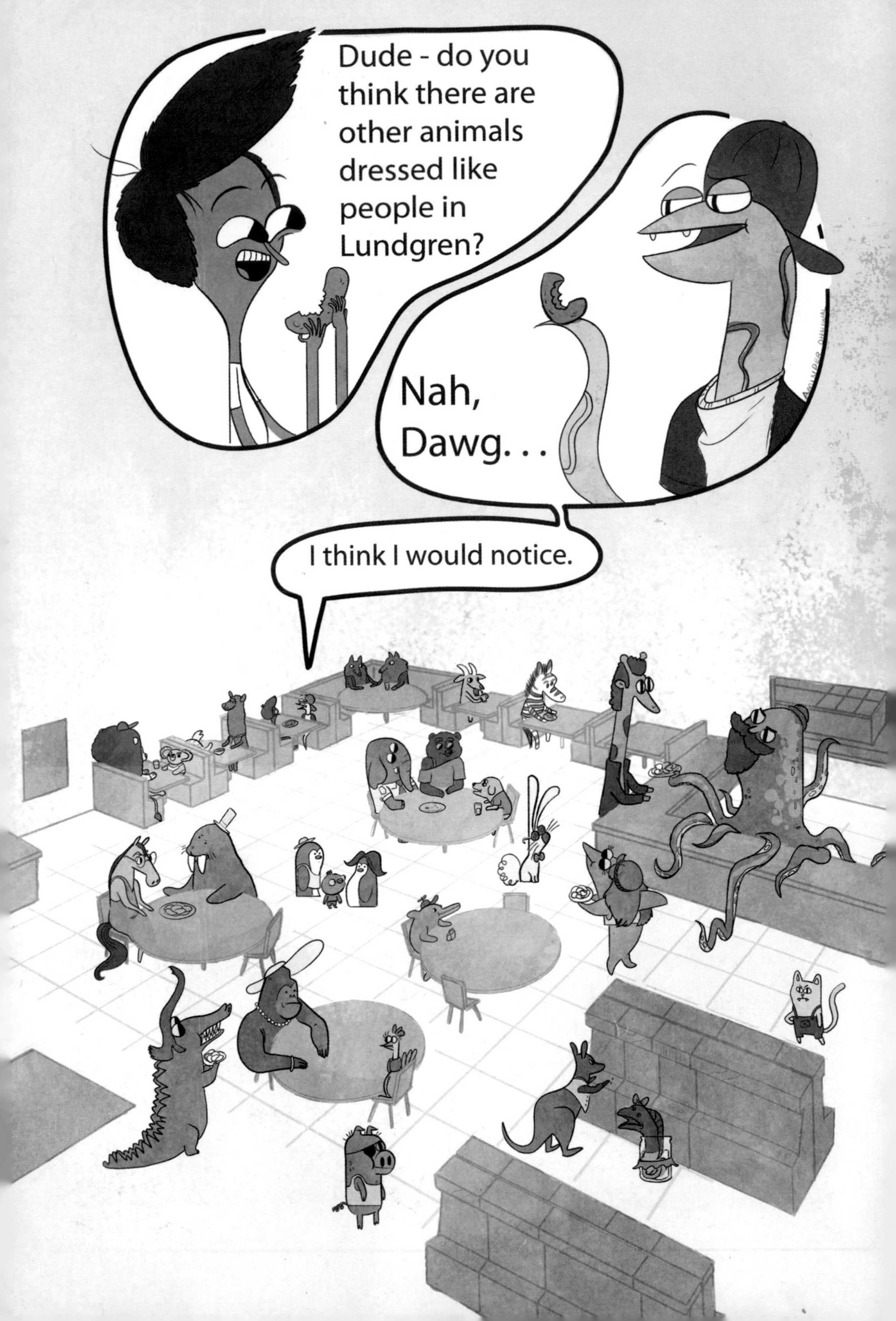
Dude - do you think there are other animals dressed like people in Lundgren?
Nah, Dawg. . .
I think I would notice.

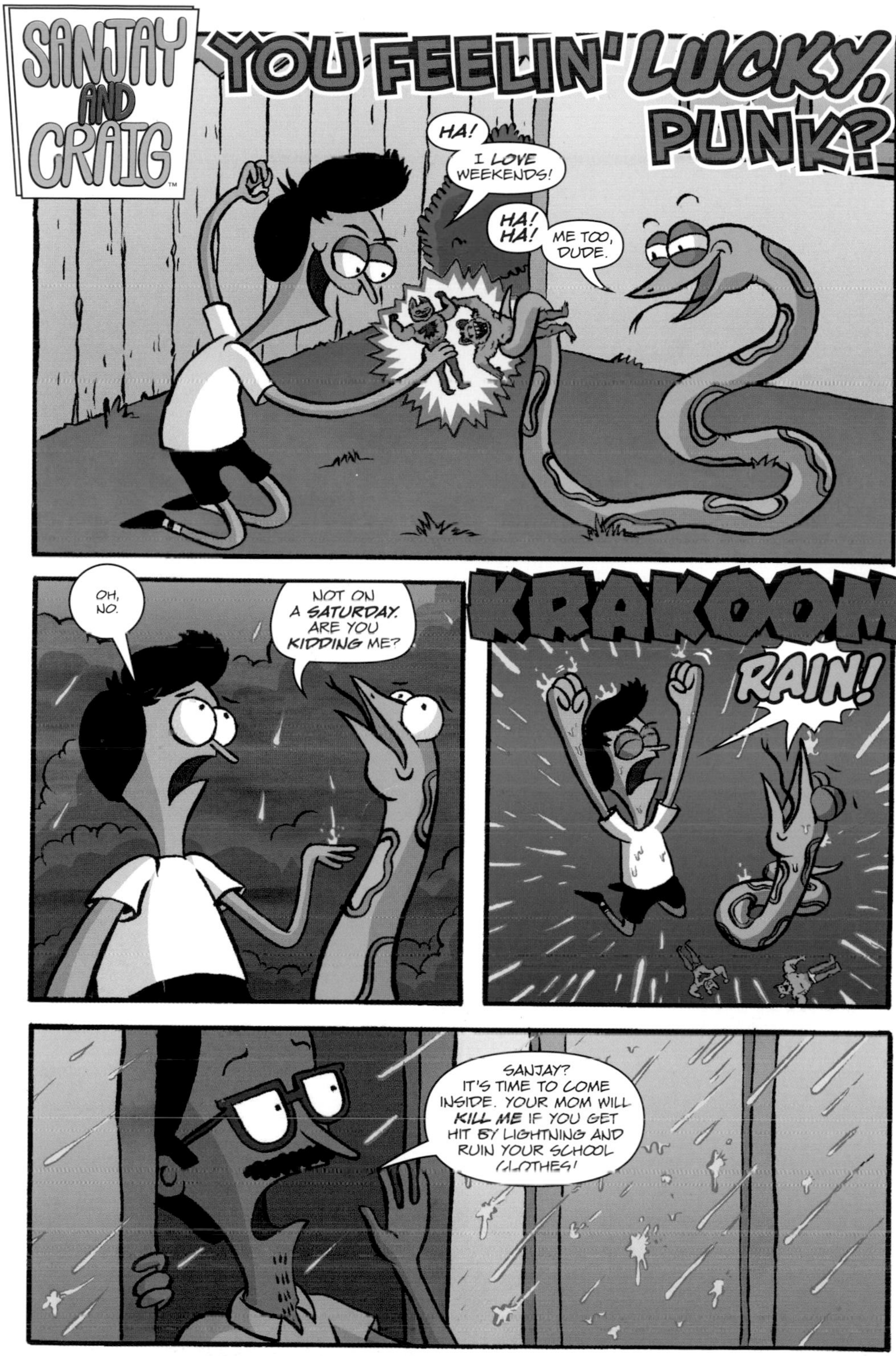
SANJAY AND CRAIG™
YOU FEELIN' LUCKY, PUNK?
HA! I LOVE WEEKENDS!
HA! HA!
ME TOO, DUDE.
OH, NO.
NOT ON A SATURDAY. ARE YOU KIDDING ME?
KRAKOOM
RAIN!
SANJAY? IT'S TIME TO COME INSIDE. YOUR MOM WILL KILL ME IF YOU GET HIT BY LIGHTNING AND RUIN YOUR SCHOOL CLOTHES!

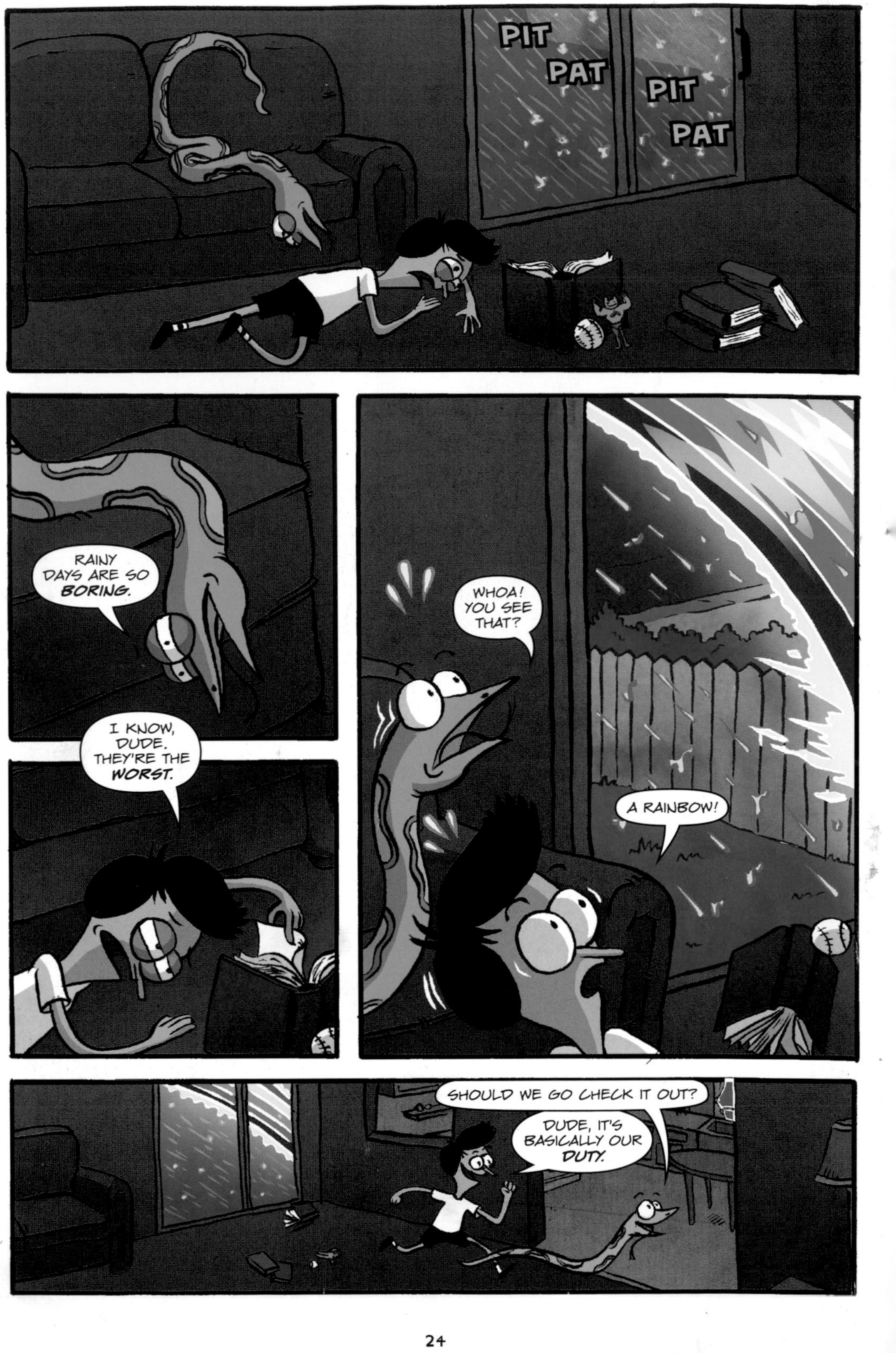
PIT
PAT
PIT
PAT
RAINY DAYS ARE SO BORING.
I KNOW, DUDE. THEY'RE THE WORST.
WHOA! YOU SEE THAT?
A RAINBOW!
SHOULD WE GO CHECK IT OUT?
DUDE, IT'S BASICALLY OUR DUTY.

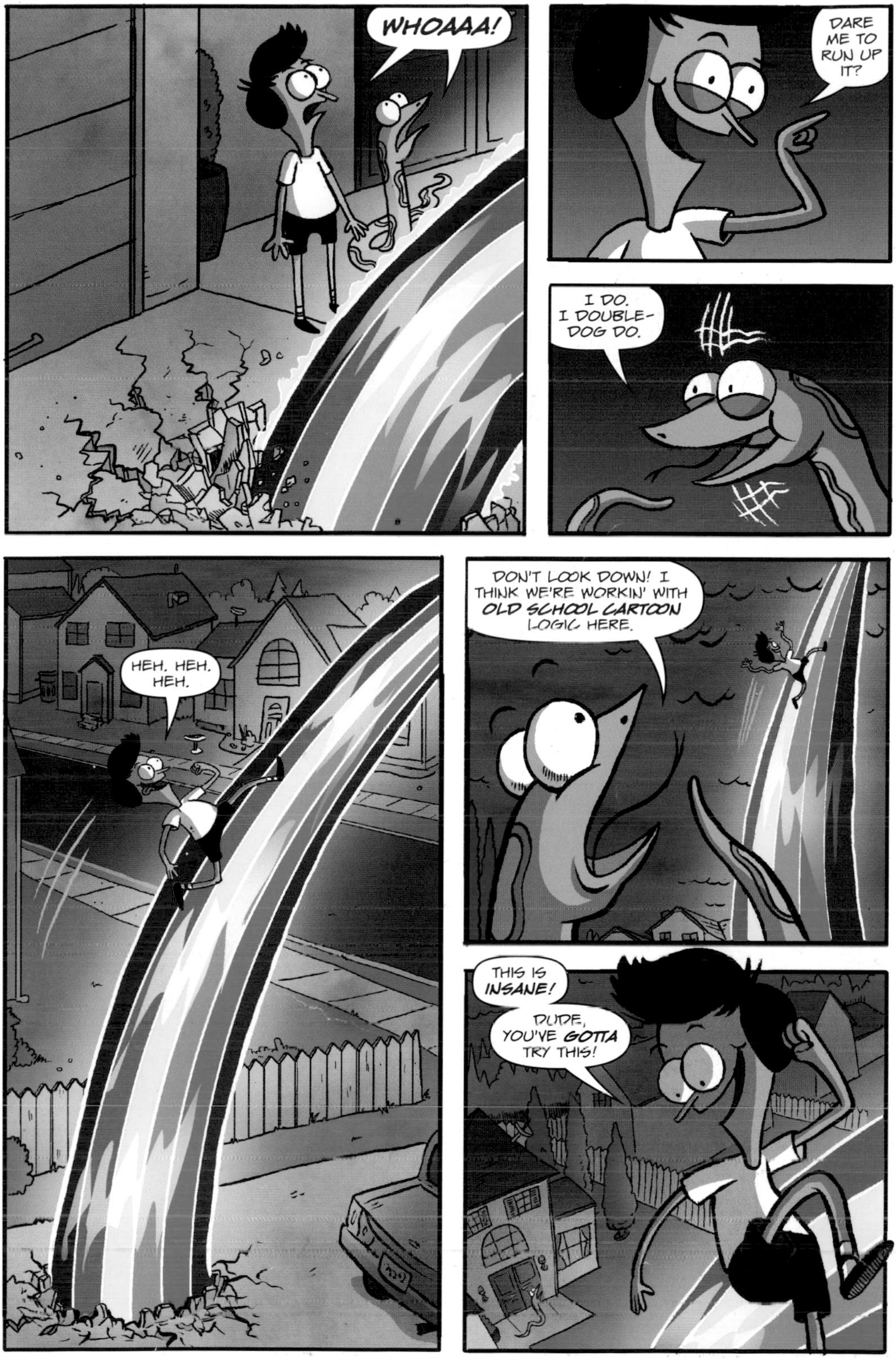
WHOAAA!
DARE ME TO RUN UP IT?
I DO. I DOUBLE-DOG DO.
HEH. HEH. HEH.
DON'T LOOK DOWN! I THINK WE'RE WORKIN' WITH OLD SCHOOL CARTOON LOGIC HERE.
THIS IS INSANE!
DUDE, YOU'VE GOTTA TRY THIS!

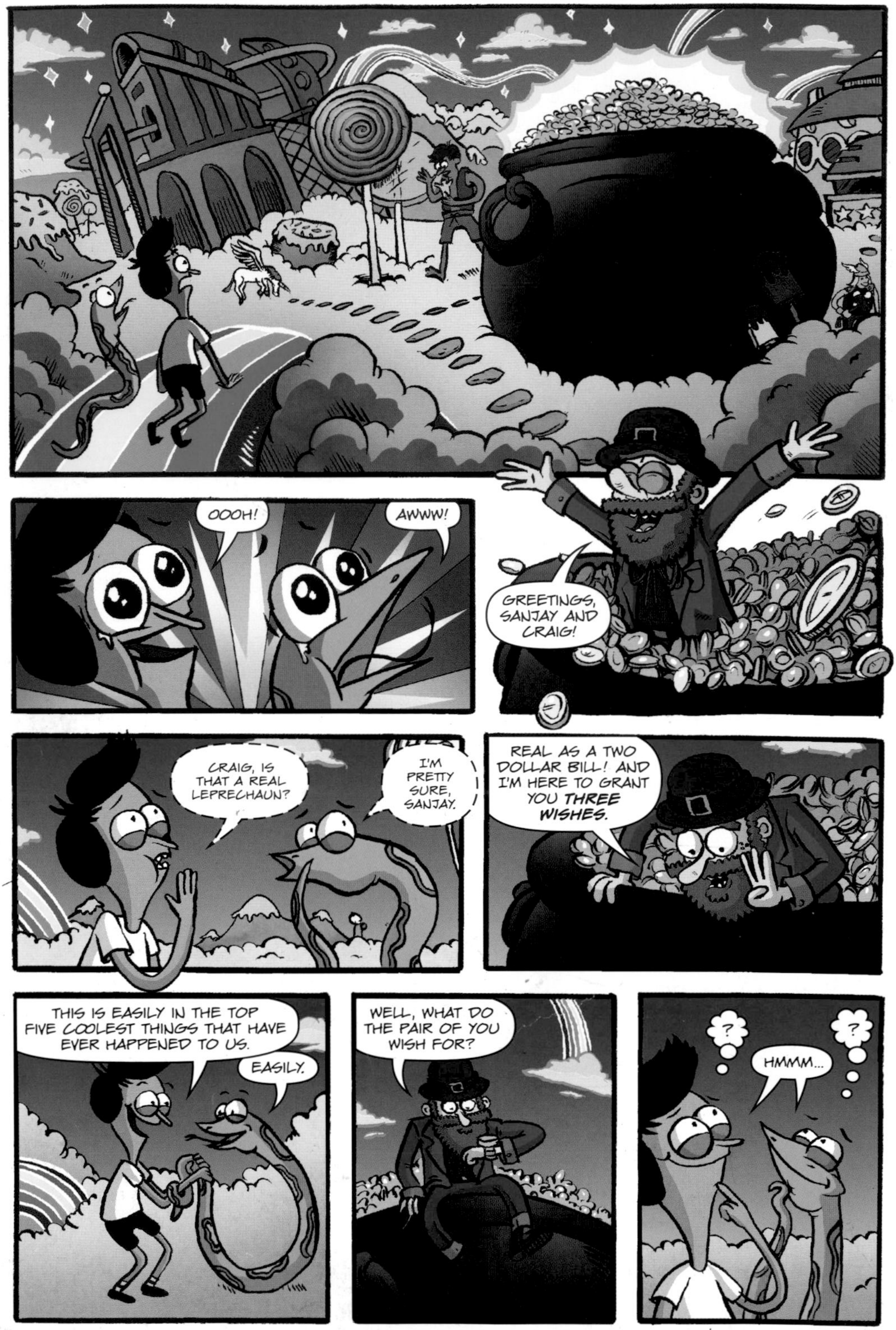
OOOH!
AWWW!
GREETINGS, SANJAY AND CRAIG!
CRAIG, IS THAT A REAL LEPRECHAUN?
I'M PRETTY SURE, SANJAY.
REAL AS A TWO DOLLAR BILL! AND I'M HERE TO GRANT YOU **THREE WISHES**.
THIS IS EASILY IN THE TOP FIVE COOLEST THINGS THAT HAVE EVER HAPPENED TO US.
EASILY.
WELL, WHAT DO THE PAIR OF YOU WISH FOR?
?
?
HMMM...

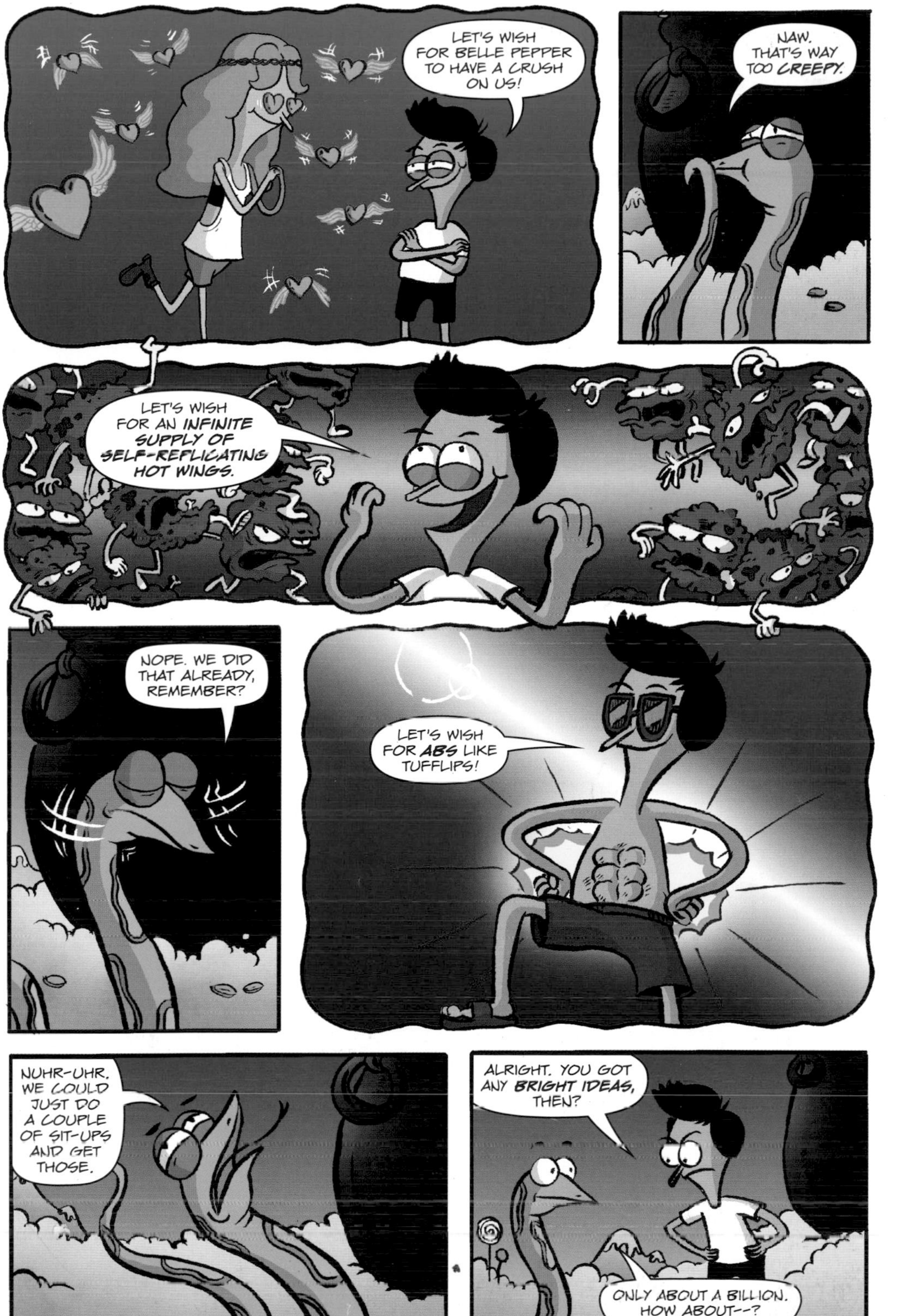
LET'S WISH FOR BELLE PEPPER TO HAVE A CRUSH ON US!
NAW. THAT'S WAY TOO CREEPY.
LET'S WISH FOR AN INFINITE SUPPLY OF SELF-REPLICATING HOT WINGS.
NOPE. WE DID THAT ALREADY, REMEMBER?
LET'S WISH FOR ABS LIKE TUFFLIPS!
NUHR-UHR. WE COULD JUST DO A COUPLE OF SIT-UPS AND GET THOSE.
ALRIGHT. YOU GOT ANY BRIGHT IDEAS, THEN?
ONLY ABOUT A BILLION. HOW ABOUT--?

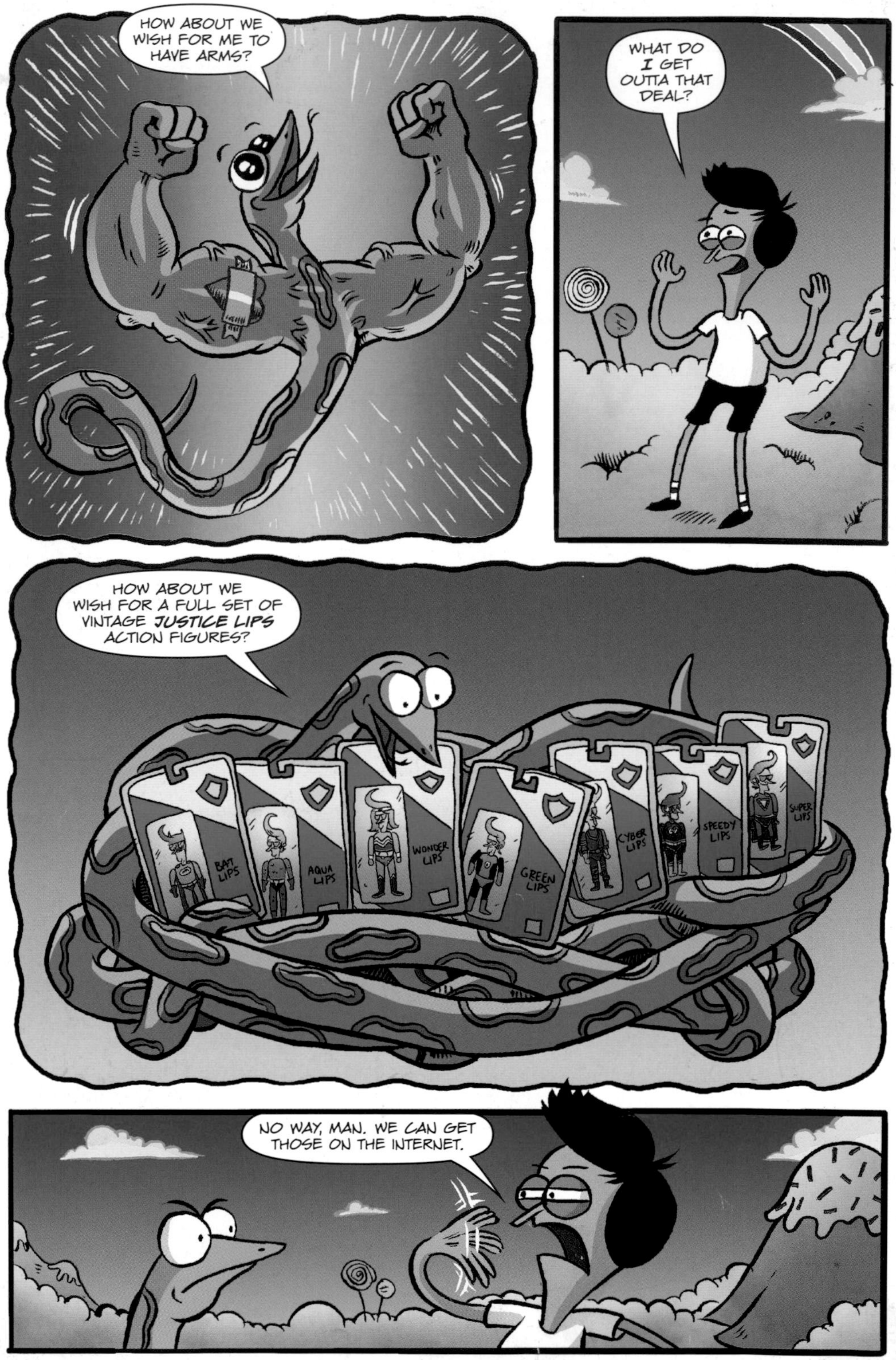
HOW ABOUT WE WISH FOR ME TO HAVE ARMS?
WHAT DO *I* GET OUTTA THAT DEAL?
HOW ABOUT WE WISH FOR A FULL SET OF VINTAGE ***JUSTICE LIPS*** ACTION FIGURES?
BAT LIPS
AQUA LIPS
WONDER LIPS
GREEN LIPS
CYBER LIPS
SPEEDY LIPS
SUPER LIPS
NO WAY, MAN. WE CAN GET THOSE ON THE INTERNET.

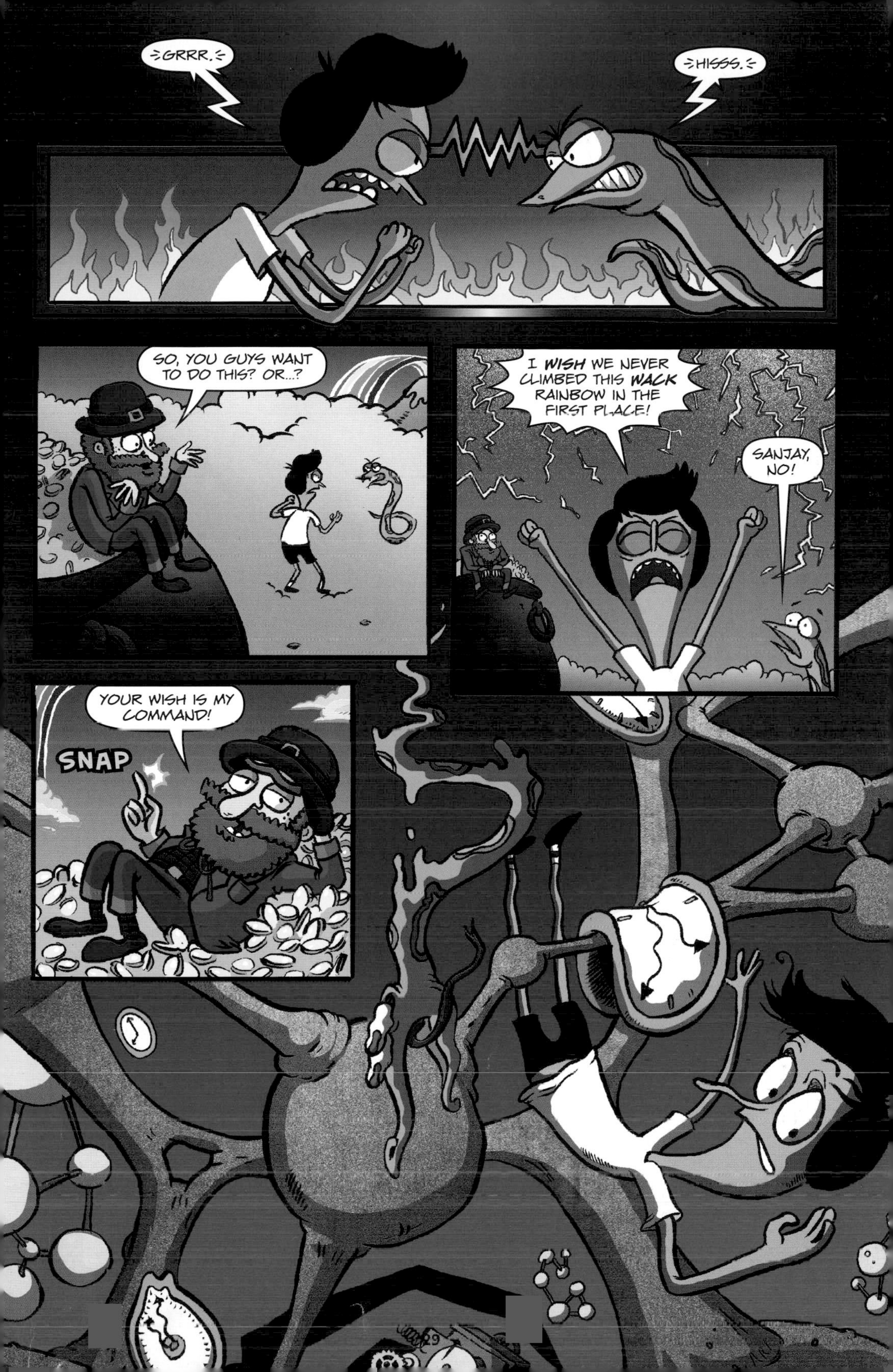
GRRR.
HISSS.
SO, YOU GUYS WANT TO DO THIS? OR...?
I WISH WE NEVER CLIMBED THIS WACK RAINBOW IN THE FIRST PLACE!
SANJAY, NO!
YOUR WISH IS MY COMMAND!
SNAP

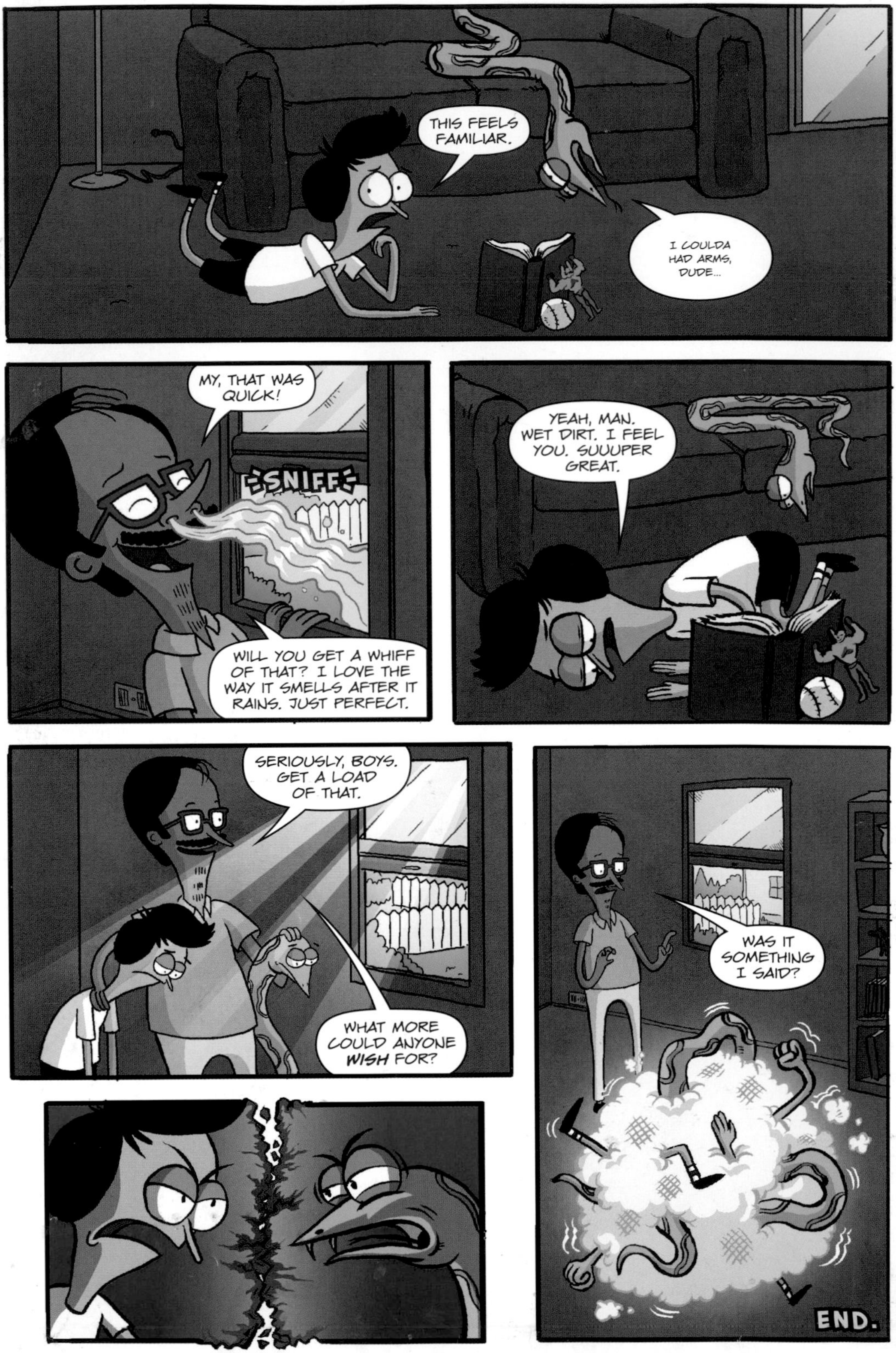
THIS FEELS FAMILIAR.
I COULDA HAD ARMS, DUDE...
MY, THAT WAS QUICK!
SNIFF
WILL YOU GET A WHIFF OF THAT? I LOVE THE WAY IT SMELLS AFTER IT RAINS. JUST PERFECT.
YEAH, MAN. WET DIRT. I FEEL YOU. SUUUPER GREAT.
SERIOUSLY, BOYS. GET A LOAD OF THAT.
WHAT MORE COULD ANYONE WISH FOR?
WAS IT SOMETHING I SAID?
END.

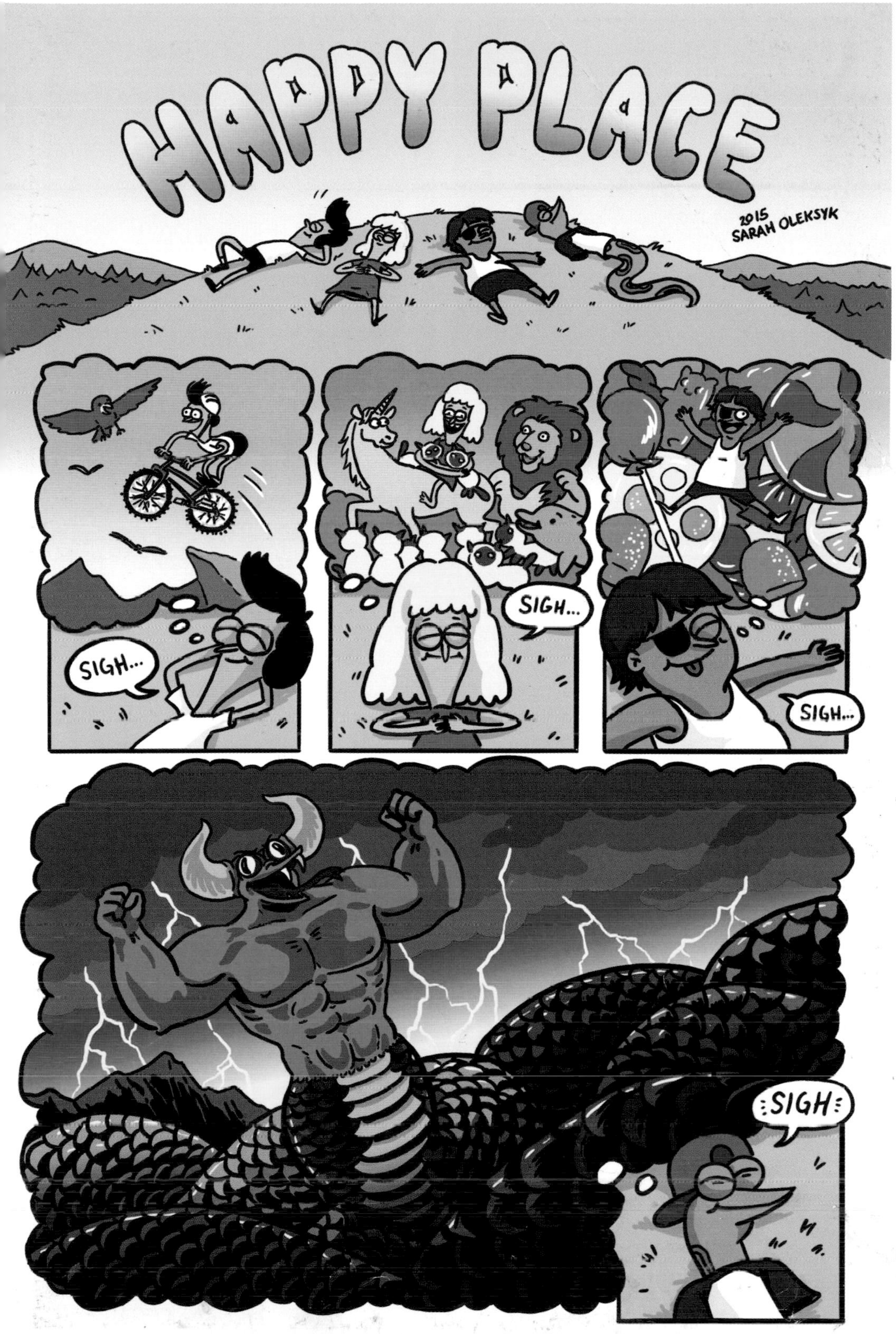
HAPPY PLACE
2015
SARAH OLEKSYK
SIGH...
SIGH...
SIGH...
SIGH

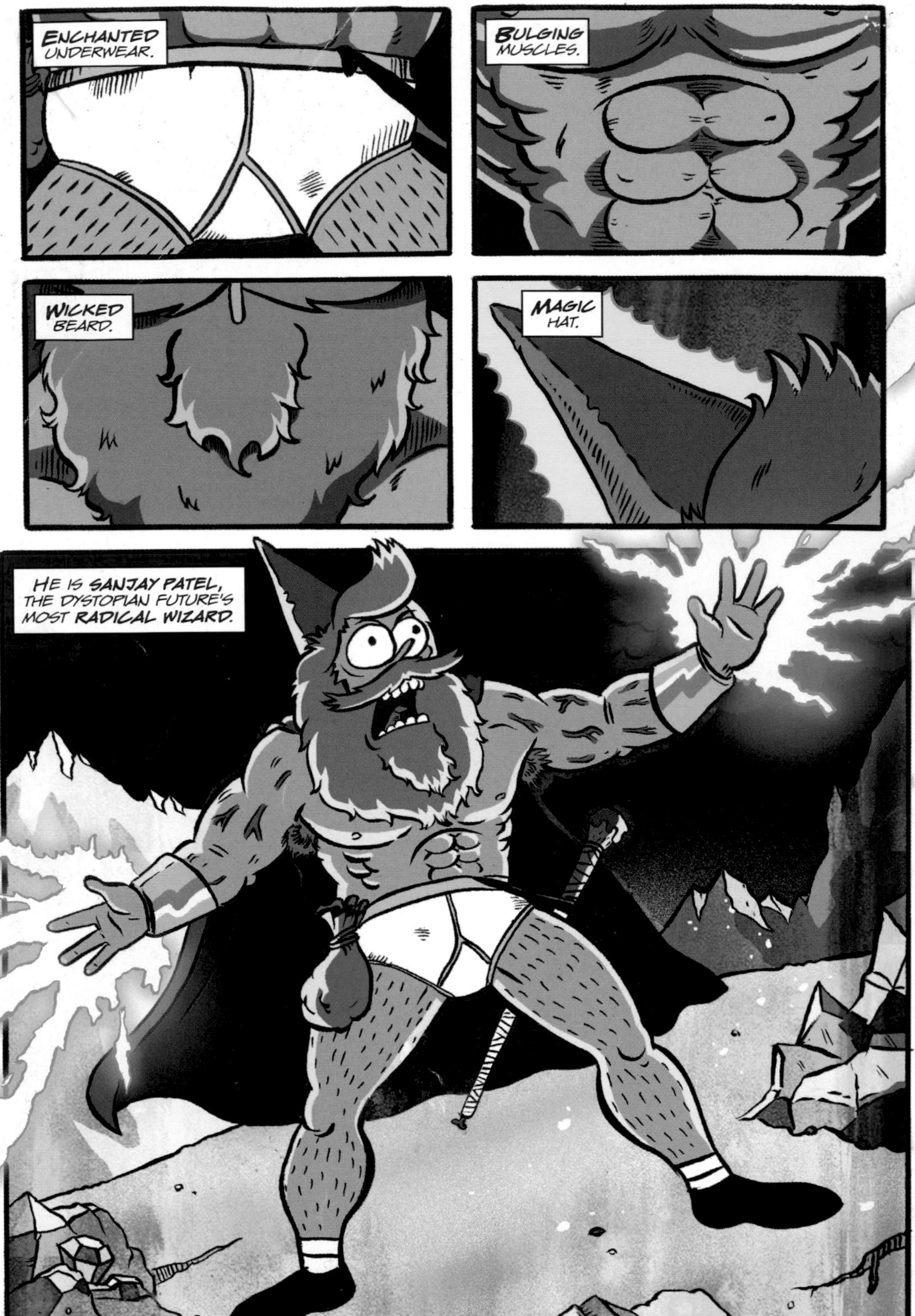
ENCHANTED UNDERWEAR.
BULGING MUSCLES.
WICKED BEARD.
MAGIC HAT.
HE IS SANJAY PATEL, THE DYSTOPIAN FUTURE'S MOST RADICAL WIZARD.

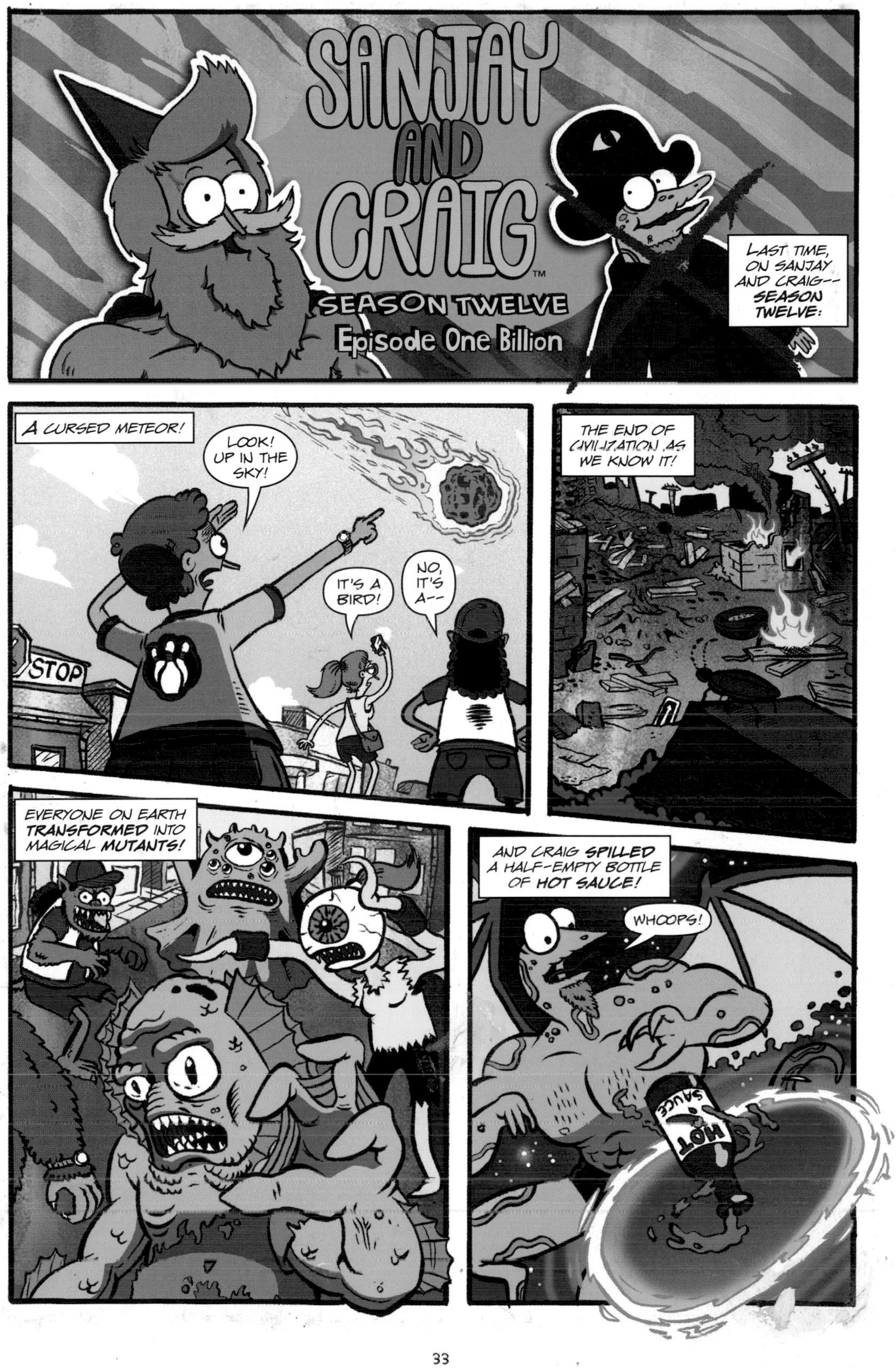
SANJAY AND CRAIG™
SEASON TWELVE
Episode One Billion
LAST TIME, ON SANJAY AND CRAIG-- SEASON TWELVE:
A CURSED METEOR!
LOOK! UP IN THE SKY!
IT'S A BIRD!
NO, IT'S A--
STOP
THE END OF CIVILIZATION AS WE KNOW IT!
EVERYONE ON EARTH TRANSFORMED INTO MAGICAL MUTANTS!
AND CRAIG SPILLED A HALF-EMPTY BOTTLE OF HOT SAUCE!
WHOOPS!
HOT SAUCE

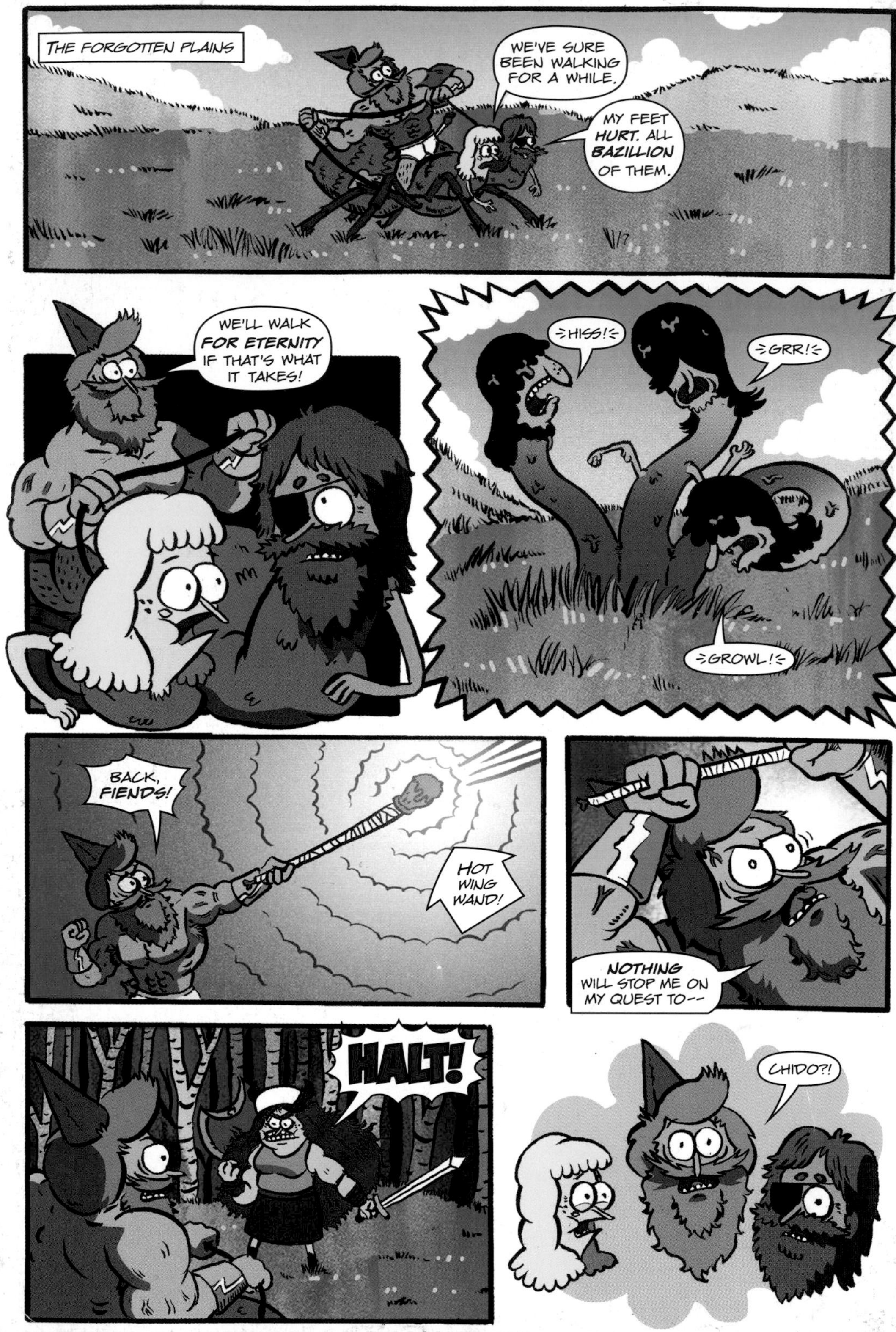
THE FORGOTTEN PLAINS
WE'VE SURE BEEN WALKING FOR A WHILE.
MY FEET HURT. ALL BAZILLION OF THEM.
WE'LL WALK FOR ETERNITY IF THAT'S WHAT IT TAKES!
HISS!
GRR!
GROWL!
BACK, FIENDS!
HOT WING WAND!
NOTHING WILL STOP ME ON MY QUEST TO--
HALT!
CHIDO?!

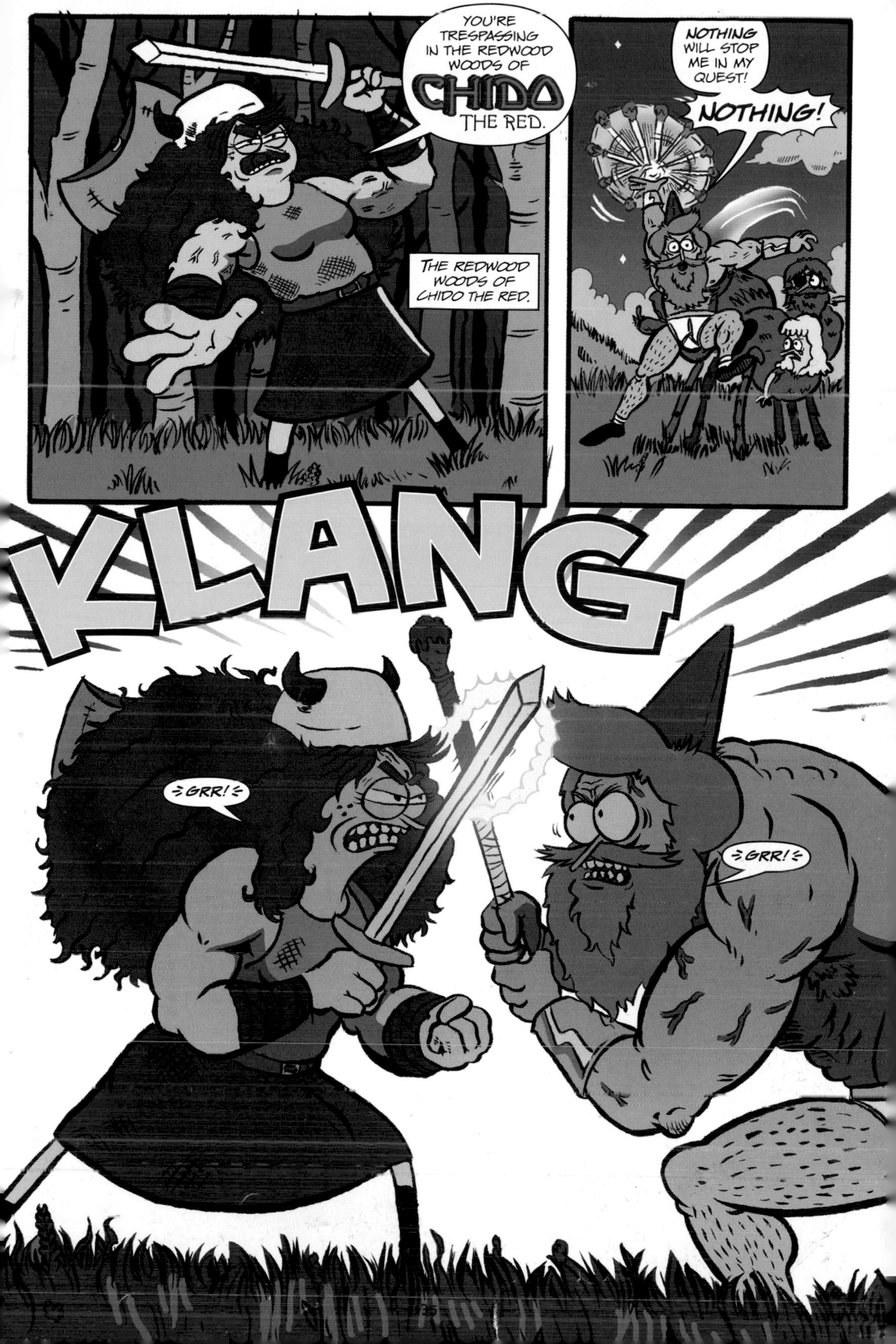
YOU'RE TRESPASSING IN THE REDWOOD WOODS OF CHIDO THE RED.
THE REDWOOD WOODS OF CHIDO THE RED.
NOTHING WILL STOP ME IN MY QUEST!
NOTHING!
KLANG
GRR!
GRR!

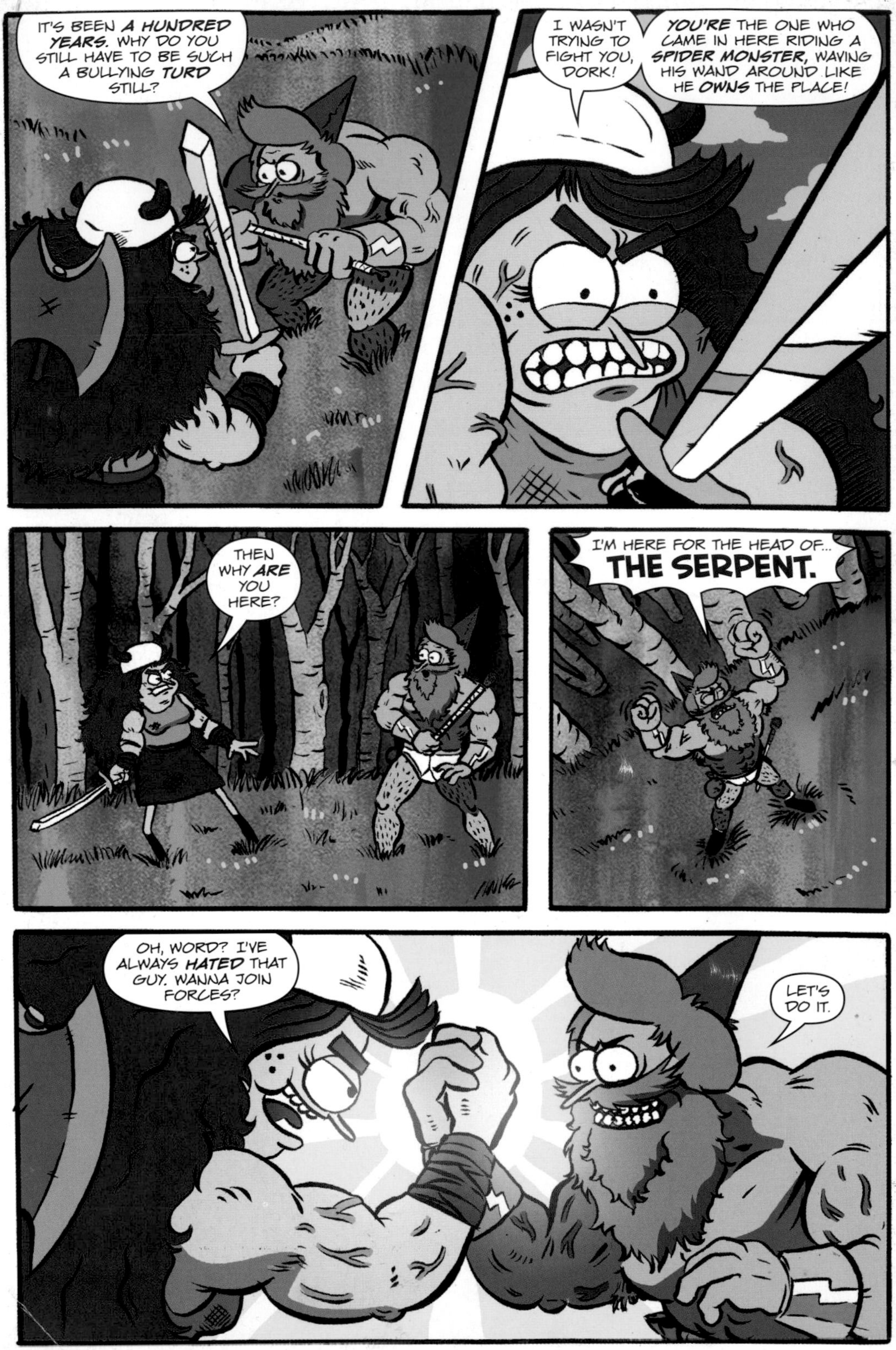
IT'S BEEN A HUNDRED YEARS. WHY DO YOU STILL HAVE TO BE SUCH A BULLYING TURD STILL?
I WASN'T TRYING TO FIGHT YOU, DORK!
YOU'RE THE ONE WHO CAME IN HERE RIDING A SPIDER MONSTER, WAVING HIS WAND AROUND LIKE HE OWNS THE PLACE!
THEN WHY ARE YOU HERE?
I'M HERE FOR THE HEAD OF... THE SERPENT.
OH, WORD? I'VE ALWAYS HATED THAT GUY. WANNA JOIN FORCES?
LET'S DO IT.

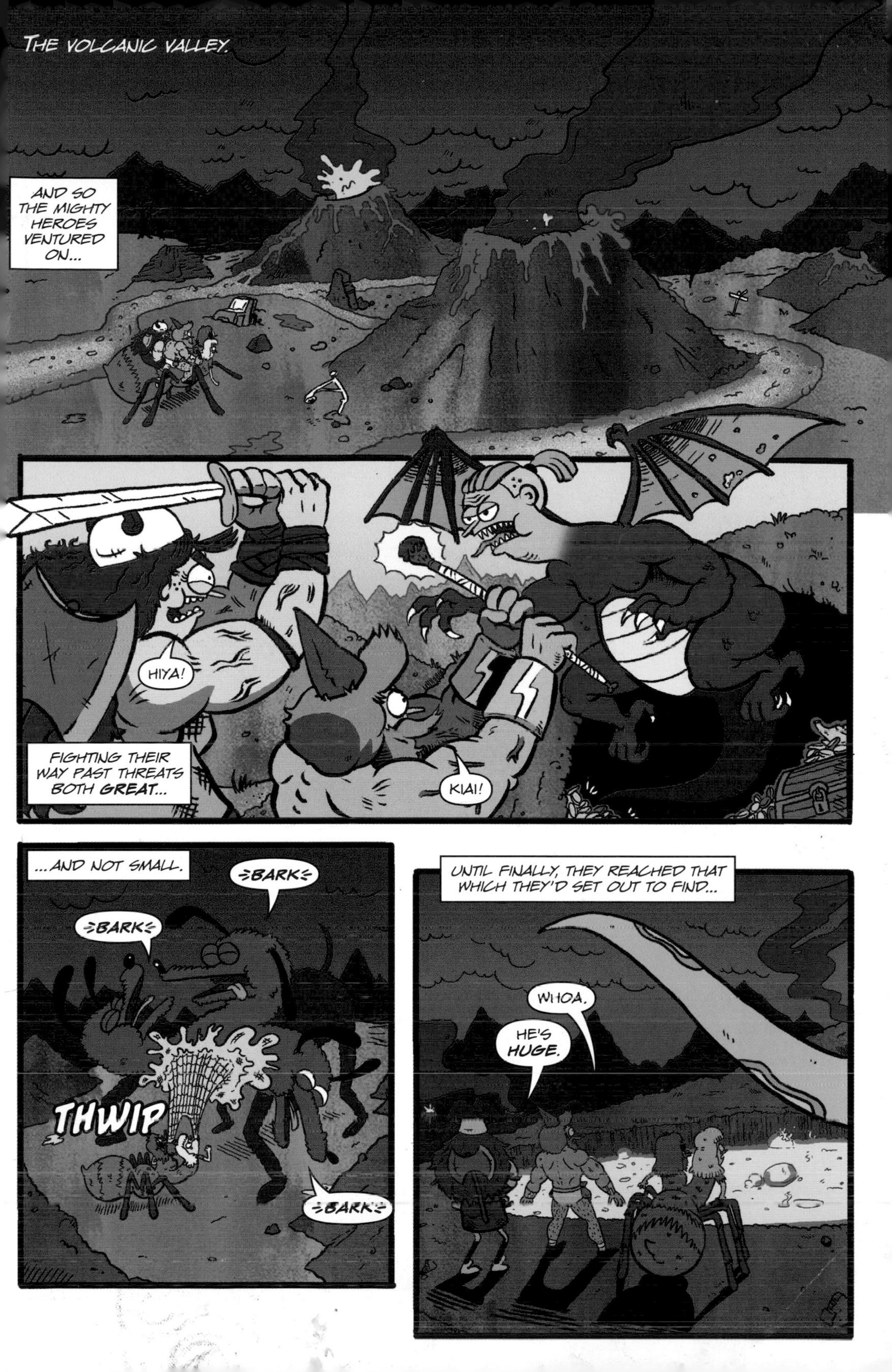
THE VOLCANIC VALLEY.
AND SO THE MIGHTY HEROES VENTURED ON...
HIYA!
FIGHTING THEIR WAY PAST THREATS BOTH GREAT...
KIAI!
...AND NOT SMALL.
BARK
BARK
THWIP
BARK
UNTIL FINALLY, THEY REACHED THAT WHICH THEY'D SET OUT TO FIND...
WHOA.
HE'S HUGE.

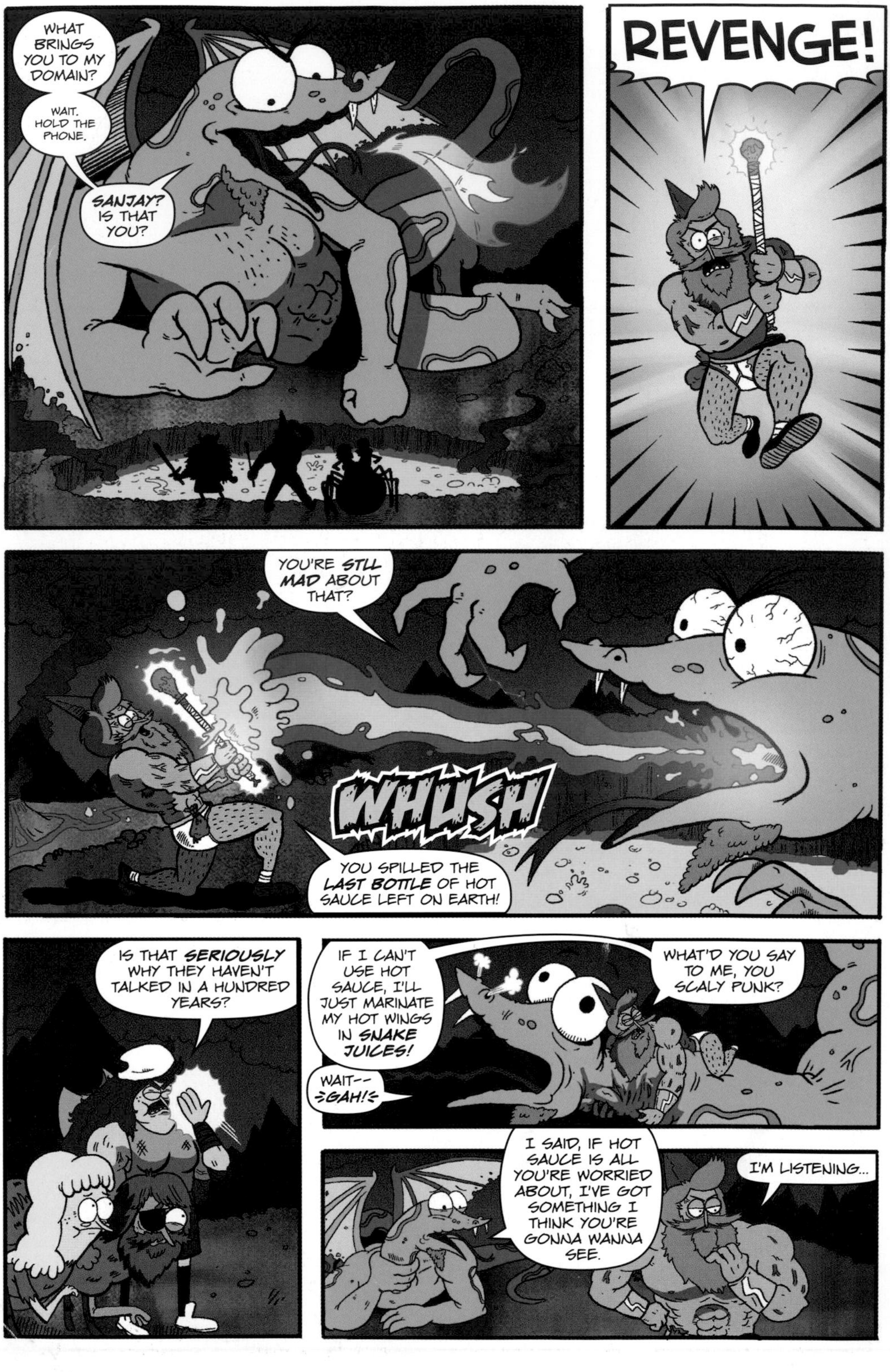
WHAT BRINGS YOU TO MY DOMAIN?
WAIT. HOLD THE PHONE.
SANJAY? IS THAT YOU?
REVENGE!
YOU'RE STILL MAD ABOUT THAT?
WHUSH
YOU SPILLED THE LAST BOTTLE OF HOT SAUCE LEFT ON EARTH!
IS THAT SERIOUSLY WHY THEY HAVEN'T TALKED IN A HUNDRED YEARS?
IF I CAN'T USE HOT SAUCE, I'LL JUST MARINATE MY HOT WINGS IN SNAKE JUICES!
WAIT-- GAH!
WHAT'D YOU SAY TO ME, YOU SCALY PUNK?
I SAID, IF HOT SAUCE IS ALL YOU'RE WORRIED ABOUT, I'VE GOT SOMETHING I THINK YOU'RE GONNA WANNA SEE.
I'M LISTENING...

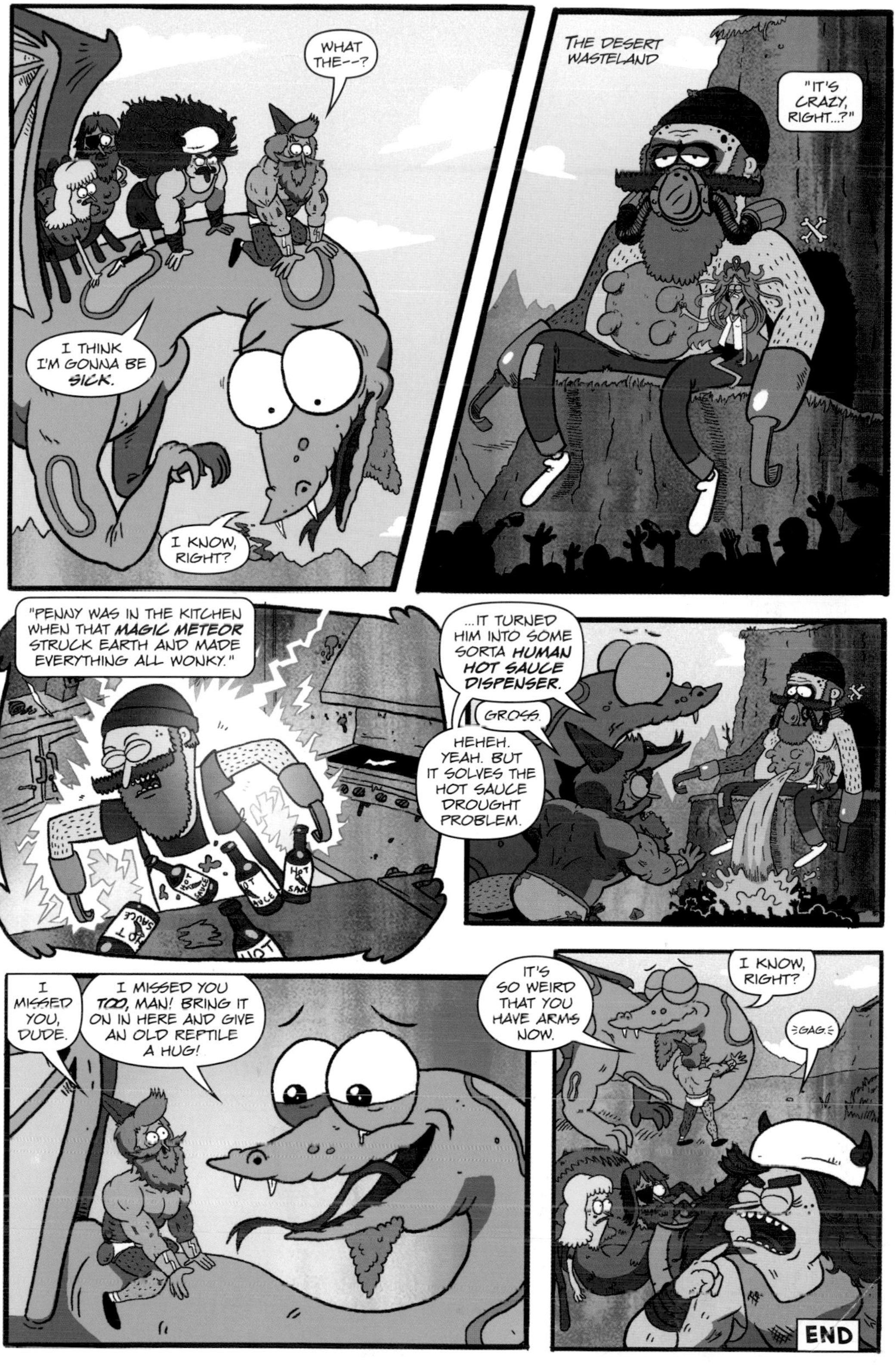
WHAT THE--?
I THINK I'M GONNA BE SICK.
I KNOW, RIGHT?
THE DESERT WASTELAND
"IT'S CRAZY, RIGHT...?"
"PENNY WAS IN THE KITCHEN WHEN THAT MAGIC METEOR STRUCK EARTH AND MADE EVERYTHING ALL WONKY."
...IT TURNED HIM INTO SOME SORTA HUMAN HOT SAUCE DISPENSER.
GROSS.
HEHEH. YEAH. BUT IT SOLVES THE HOT SAUCE DROUGHT PROBLEM.
I MISSED YOU, DUDE.
I MISSED YOU TOO, MAN! BRING IT ON IN HERE AND GIVE AN OLD REPTILE A HUG!
IT'S SO WEIRD THAT YOU HAVE ARMS NOW.
I KNOW, RIGHT?
GAG.
END

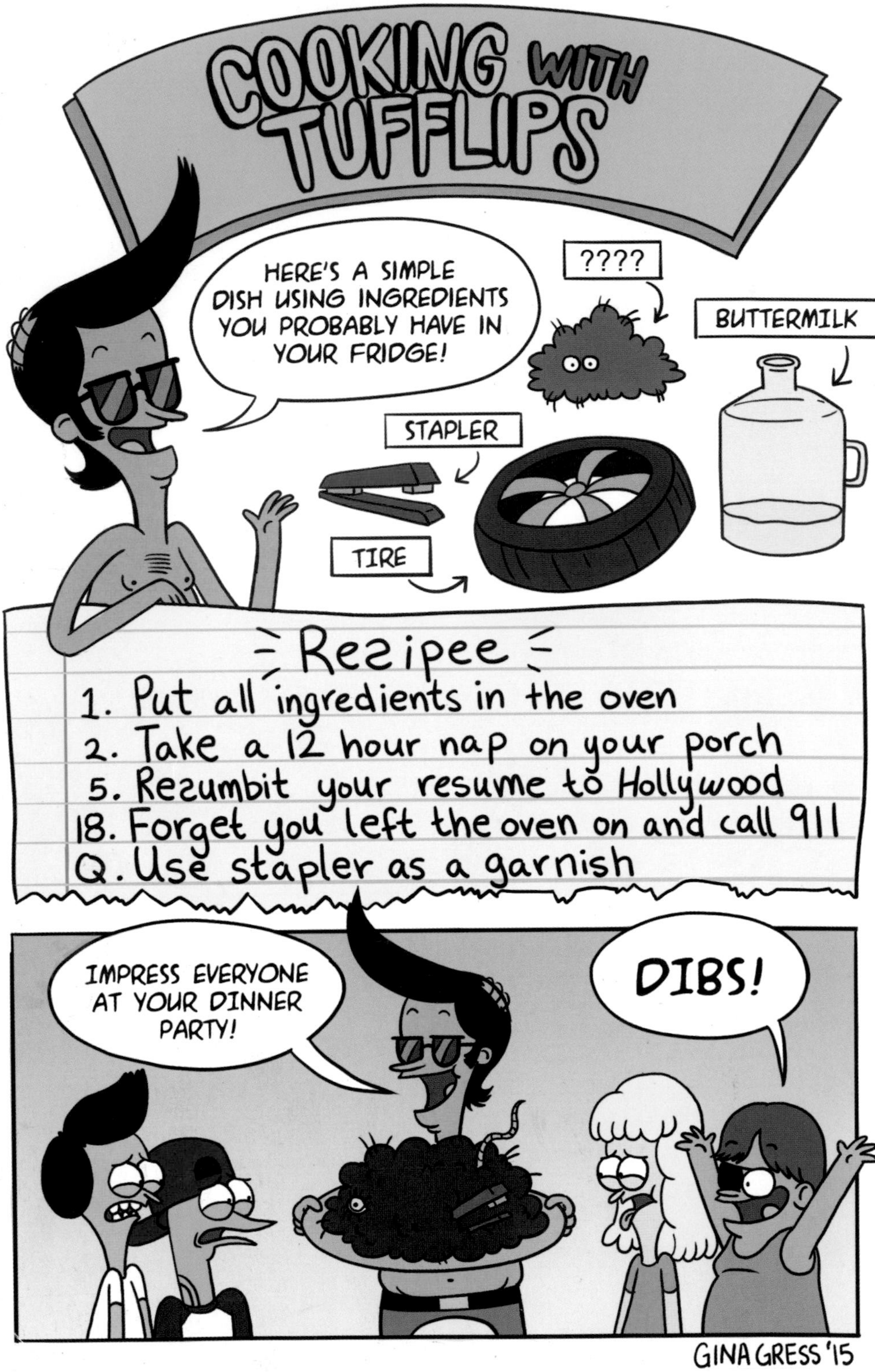
COOKING WITH TUFFLIPS
HERE'S A SIMPLE DISH USING INGREDIENTS YOU PROBABLY HAVE IN YOUR FRIDGE!
????
BUTTERMILK
STAPLER
TIRE
Rezipee
1. Put all ingredients in the oven
2. Take a 12 hour nap on your porch
5. Rezumbit your resume to Hollywood
18. Forget you left the oven on and call 911
Q. Use stapler as a garnish
IMPRESS EVERYONE AT YOUR DINNER PARTY!
DIBS!
GINA GRESS '15

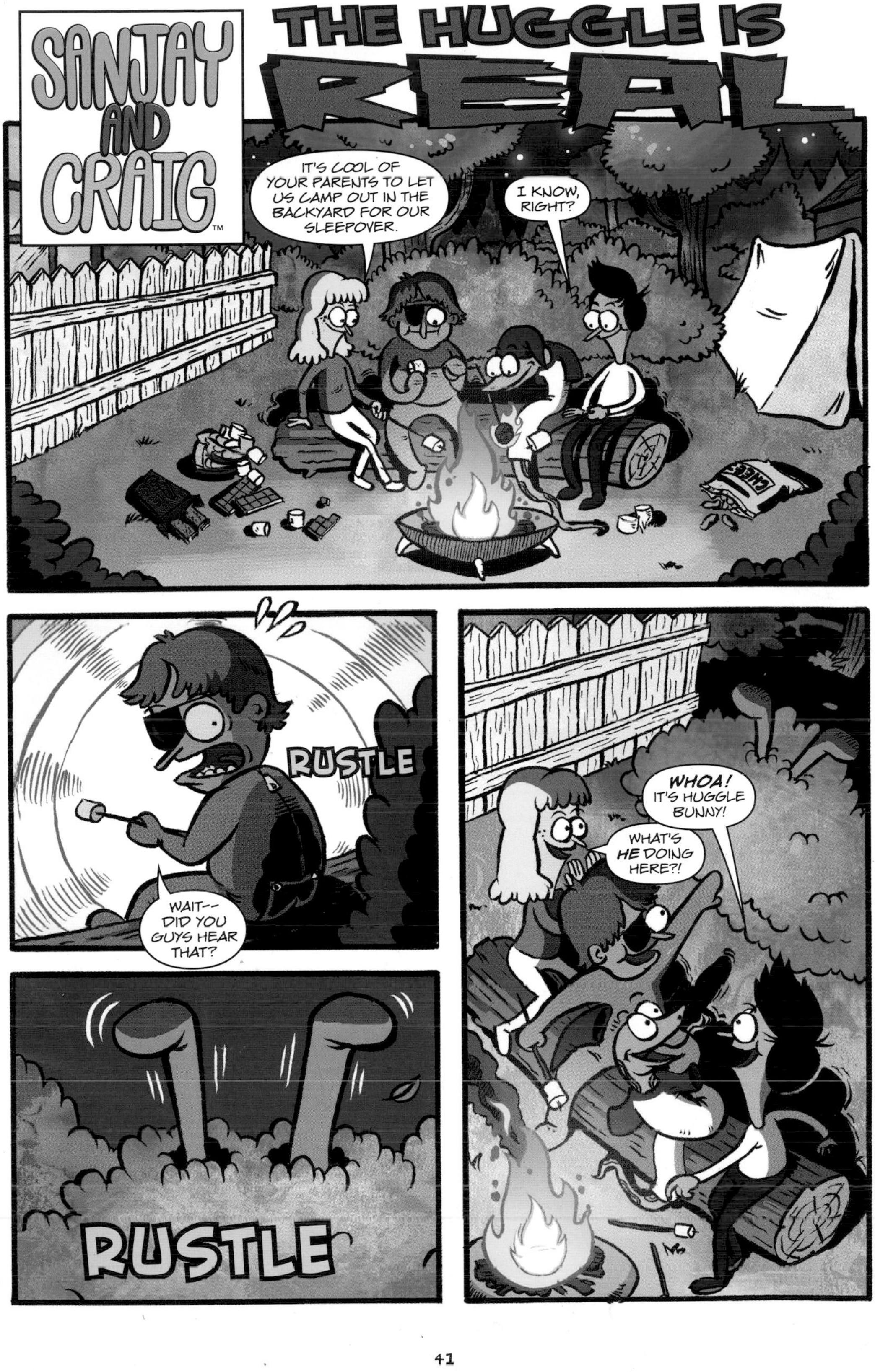
SANJAY AND CRAIG™
THE HUGGLE IS REAL
IT'S COOL OF YOUR PARENTS TO LET US CAMP OUT IN THE BACKYARD FOR OUR SLEEPOVER.
I KNOW, RIGHT?
RUSTLE
WAIT-- DID YOU GUYS HEAR THAT?
RUSTLE
WHOA! IT'S HUGGLE BUNNY!
WHAT'S HE DOING HERE?!

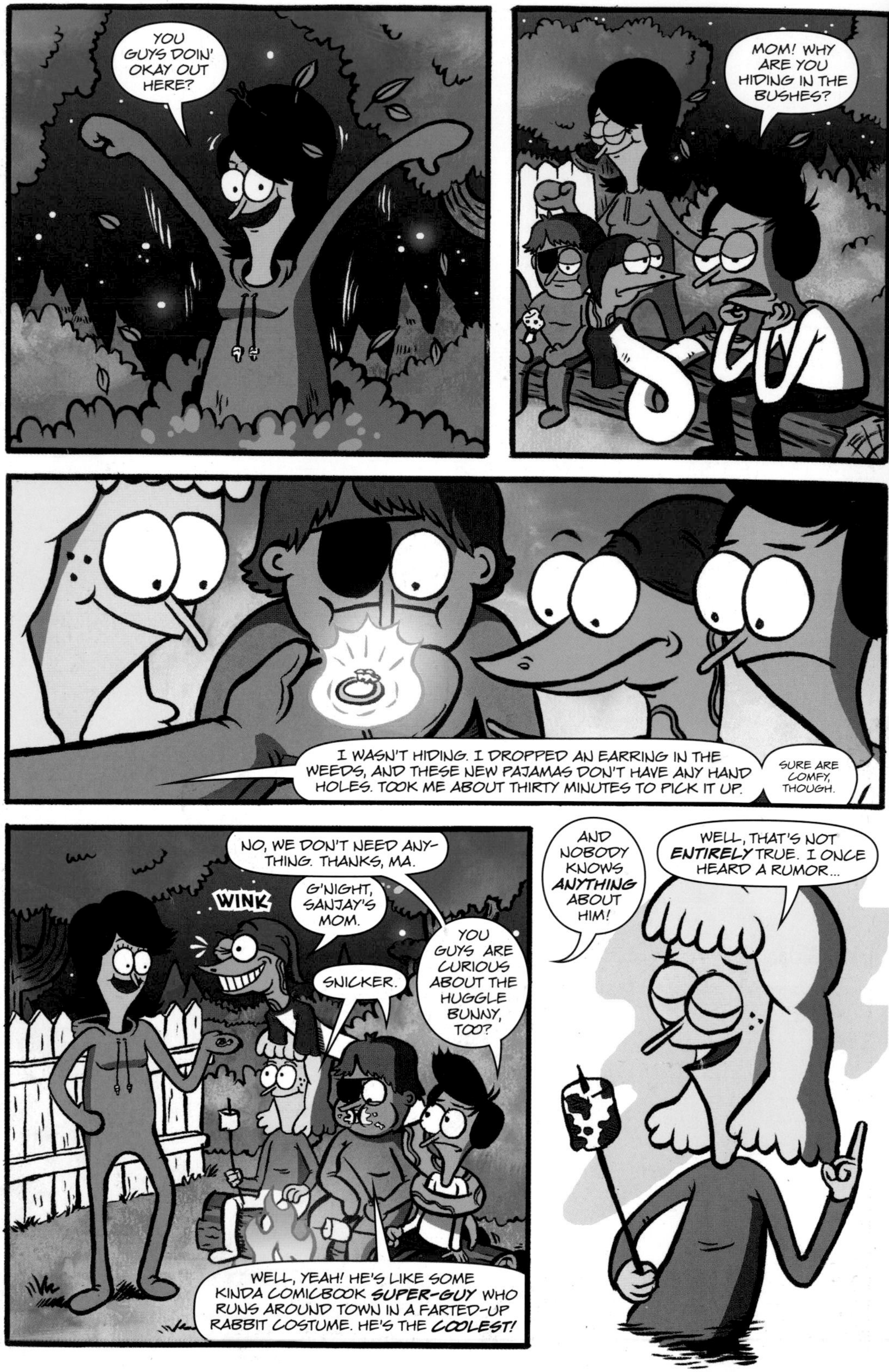
YOU GUYS DOIN' OKAY OUT HERE?
MOM! WHY ARE YOU HIDING IN THE BUSHES?
I WASN'T HIDING. I DROPPED AN EARRING IN THE WEEDS, AND THESE NEW PAJAMAS DON'T HAVE ANY HAND HOLES. TOOK ME ABOUT THIRTY MINUTES TO PICK IT UP.
SURE ARE COMFY, THOUGH.
NO, WE DON'T NEED ANY-THING. THANKS, MA.
WINK
G'NIGHT, SANJAY'S MOM.
YOU GUYS ARE CURIOUS ABOUT THE HUGGLE BUNNY, TOO?
SNICKER.
WELL, YEAH! HE'S LIKE SOME KINDA COMICBOOK SUPER-GUY WHO RUNS AROUND TOWN IN A FARTED-UP RABBIT COSTUME. HE'S THE COOLEST!
AND NOBODY KNOWS ANYTHING ABOUT HIM!
WELL, THAT'S NOT ENTIRELY TRUE. I ONCE HEARD A RUMOR...

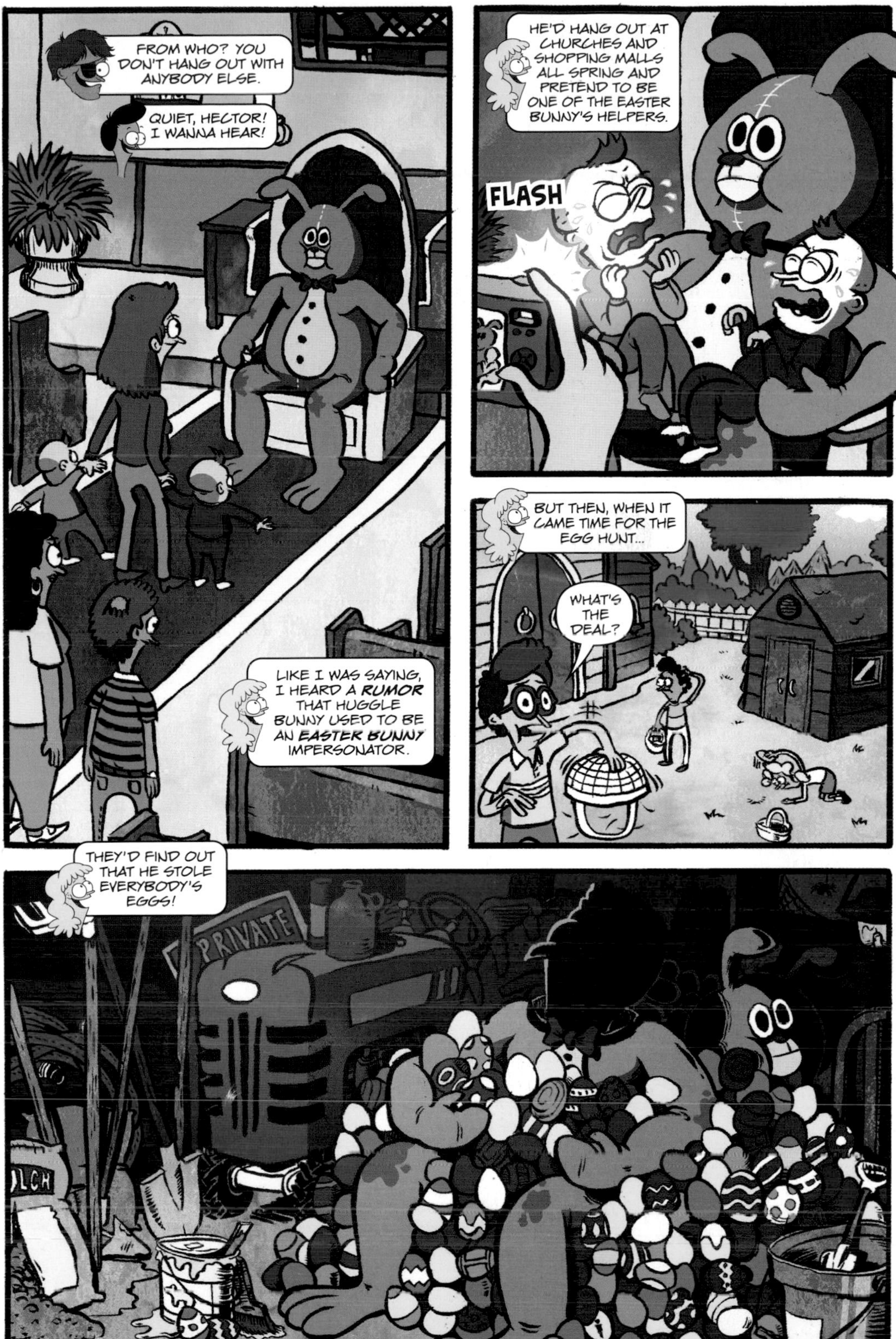

FROM WHO? YOU DON'T HANG OUT WITH ANYBODY ELSE.
QUIET, HECTOR! I WANNA HEAR!
LIKE I WAS SAYING, I HEARD A **RUMOR** THAT HUGGLE BUNNY USED TO BE AN **EASTER BUNNY** IMPERSONATOR.
HE'D HANG OUT AT CHURCHES AND SHOPPING MALLS ALL SPRING AND PRETEND TO BE ONE OF THE EASTER BUNNY'S HELPERS.
FLASH
BUT THEN, WHEN IT CAME TIME FOR THE EGG HUNT...
WHAT'S THE DEAL?
THEY'D FIND OUT THAT HE STOLE EVERYBODY'S EGGS!
PRIVATE

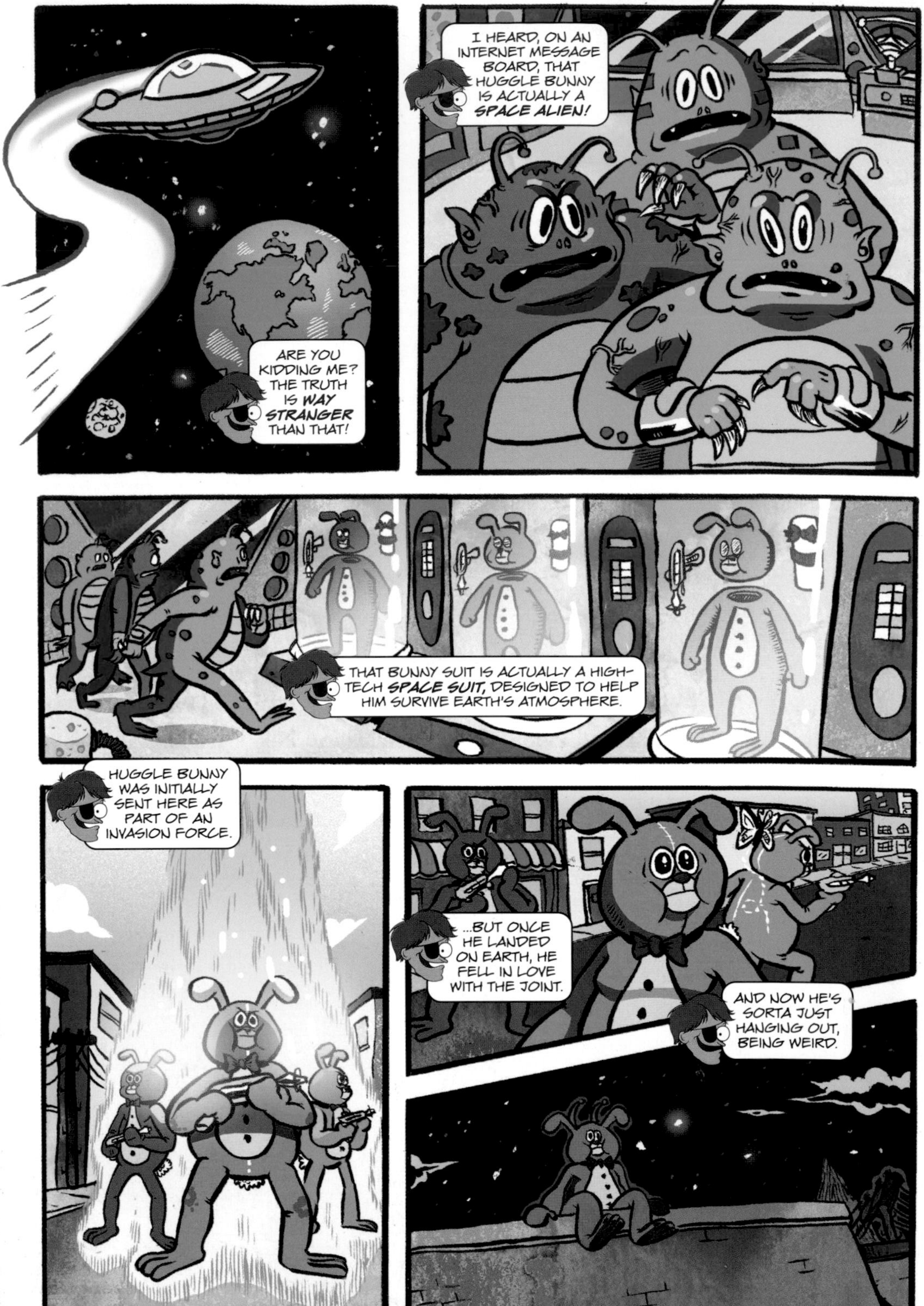
ARE YOU KIDDING ME? THE TRUTH IS WAY STRANGER THAN THAT!
I HEARD, ON AN INTERNET MESSAGE BOARD, THAT HUGGLE BUNNY IS ACTUALLY A SPACE ALIEN!
THAT BUNNY SUIT IS ACTUALLY A HIGH-TECH SPACE SUIT, DESIGNED TO HELP HIM SURVIVE EARTH'S ATMOSPHERE.
HUGGLE BUNNY WAS INITIALLY SENT HERE AS PART OF AN INVASION FORCE.
...BUT ONCE HE LANDED ON EARTH, HE FELL IN LOVE WITH THE JOINT.
AND NOW HE'S SORTA JUST HANGING OUT, BEING WEIRD.

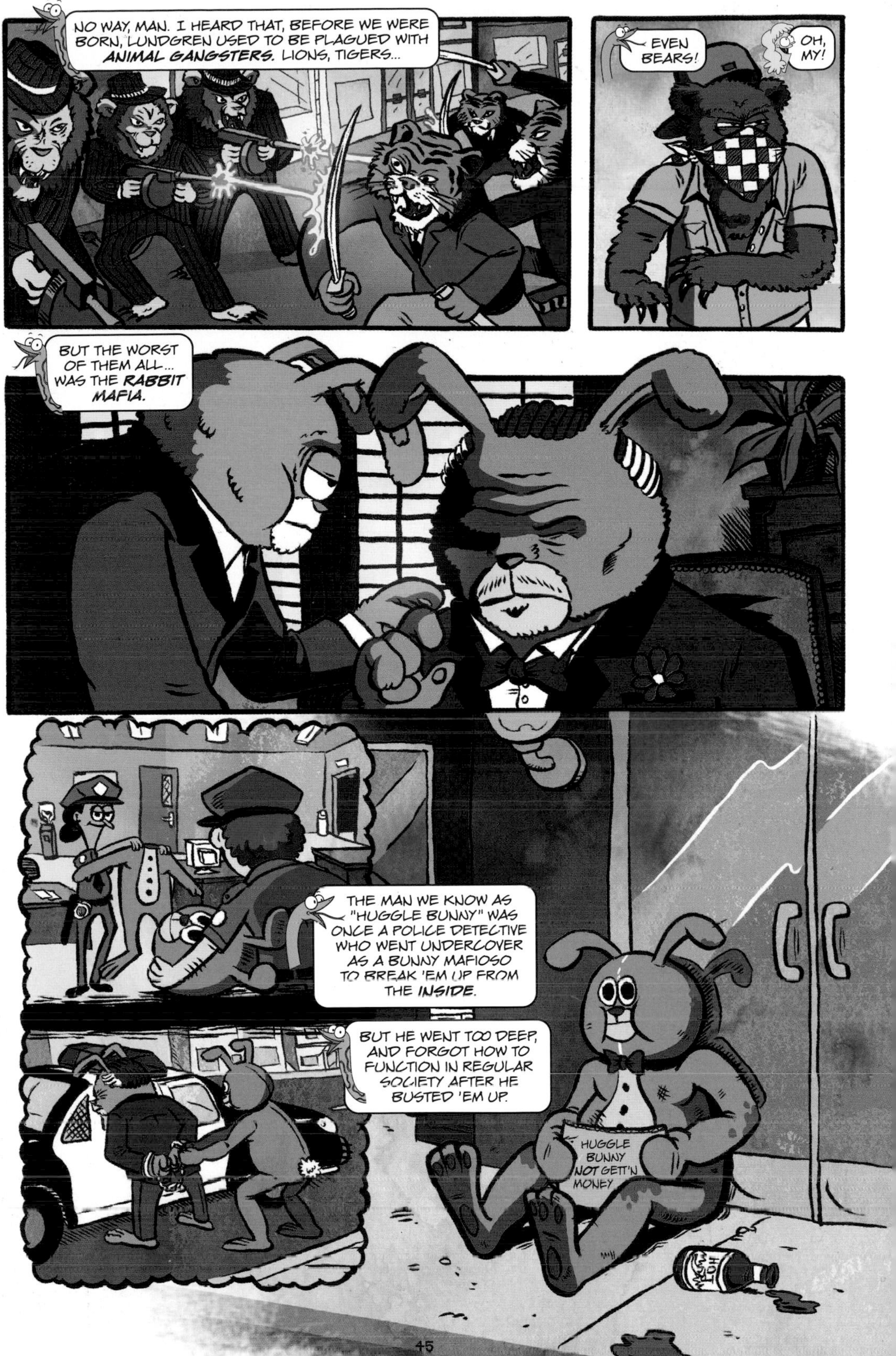
NO WAY, MAN. I HEARD THAT, BEFORE WE WERE BORN, LUNDGREN USED TO BE PLAGUED WITH ANIMAL GANGSTERS. LIONS, TIGERS...
EVEN BEARS!
OH, MY!
BUT THE WORST OF THEM ALL... WAS THE RABBIT MAFIA.
THE MAN WE KNOW AS "HUGGLE BUNNY" WAS ONCE A POLICE DETECTIVE WHO WENT UNDERCOVER AS A BUNNY MAFIOSO TO BREAK 'EM UP FROM THE INSIDE.
BUT HE WENT TOO DEEP, AND FORGOT HOW TO FUNCTION IN REGULAR SOCIETY AFTER HE BUSTED 'EM UP.
HUGGLE BUNNY NOT GETT'N MONEY

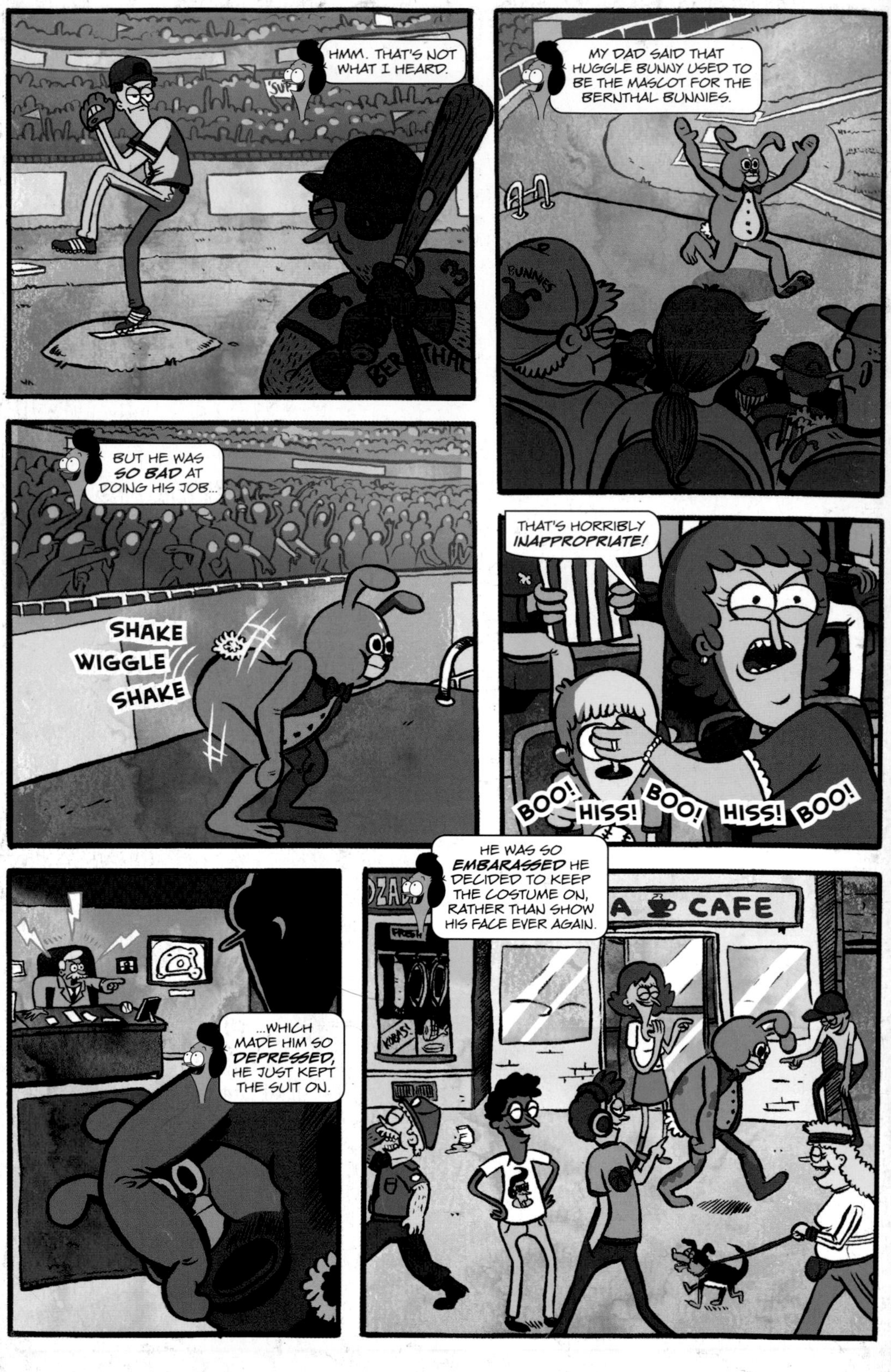
HMM. THAT'S NOT WHAT I HEARD.
'SUP
BERNTHAL
MY DAD SAID THAT HUGGLE BUNNY USED TO BE THE MASCOT FOR THE BERNTHAL BUNNIES.
BUNNIES
BUT HE WAS SO BAD AT DOING HIS JOB...
SHAKE
WIGGLE
SHAKE
THAT'S HORRIBLY INAPPROPRIATE!
BOO!
HISS!
BOO!
HISS!
BOO!
...WHICH MADE HIM SO DEPRESSED, HE JUST KEPT THE SUIT ON.
HE WAS SO EMBARASSED HE DECIDED TO KEEP THE COSTUME ON, RATHER THAN SHOW HIS FACE EVER AGAIN.
A CAFE

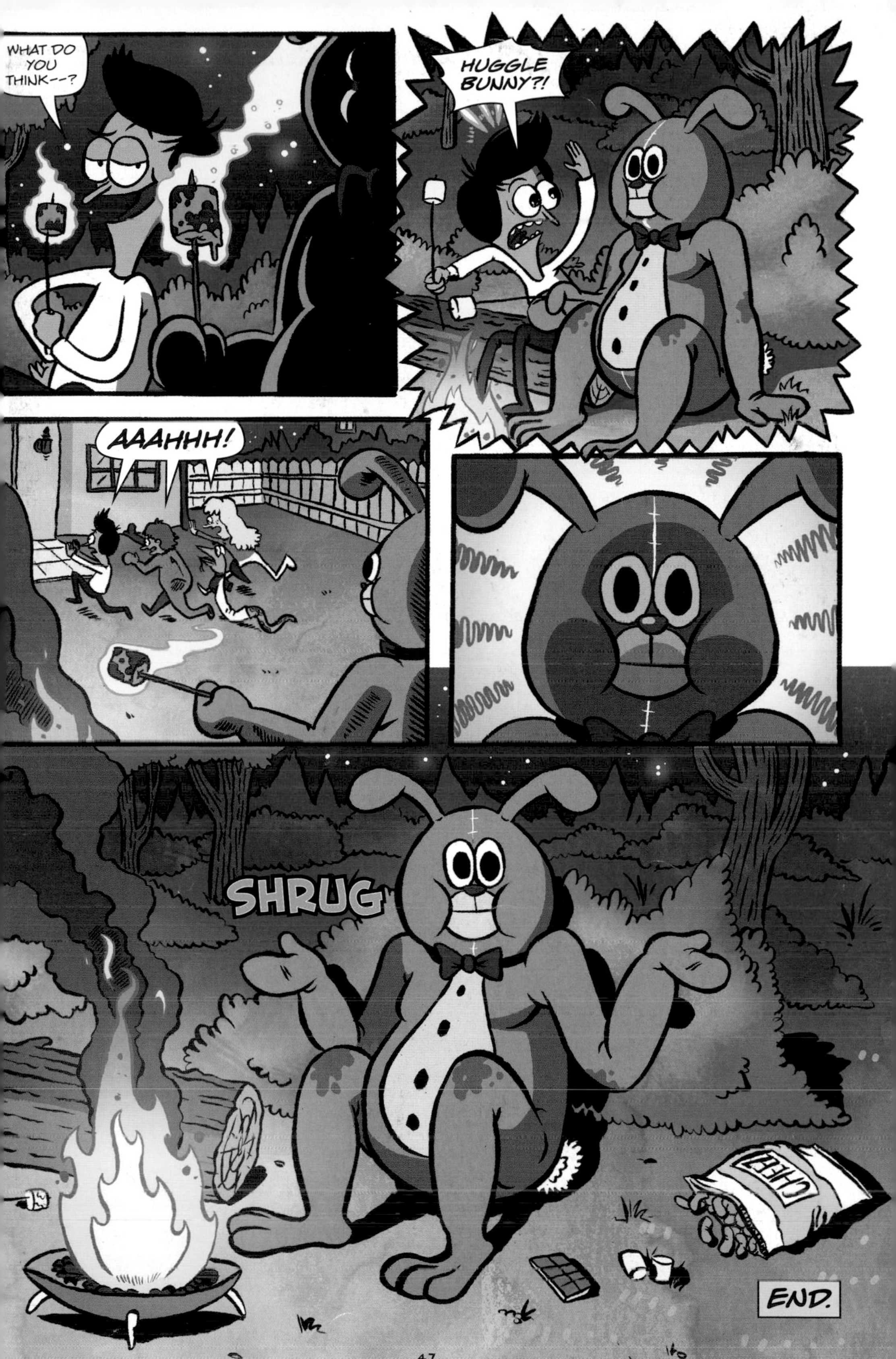
WHAT DO YOU THINK--?
HUGGLE BUNNY?!
AAAHHH!
SHRUG
END.

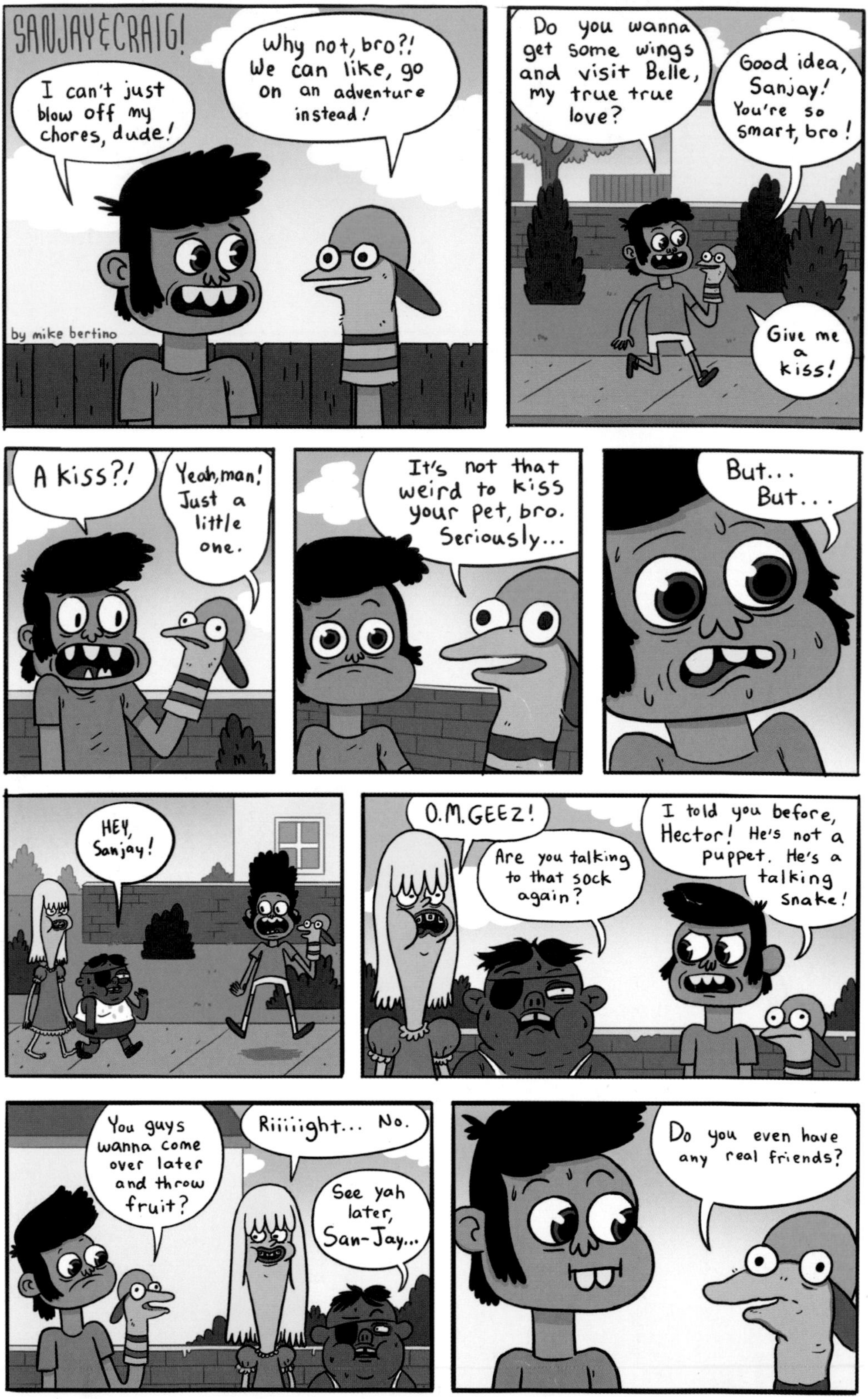
SANJAY & CRAIG!
I can't just blow off my chores, dude!
Why not, bro?! We can like, go on an adventure instead!
by mike bertino
Do you wanna get some wings and visit Belle, my true true love?
Good idea, Sanjay! You're so smart, bro!
Give me a kiss!
A kiss?!
Yeah, man! Just a little one.
It's not that weird to kiss your pet, bro. Seriously...
But... But...
HEY, Sanjay!
O.M.GEEZ!
Are you talking to that sock again?
I told you before, Hector! He's not a puppet. He's a talking snake!
You guys wanna come over later and throw fruit?
Riiiiight... No.
See yah later, San-Jay...
Do you even have any real friends?

WATCH OUT FOR PAPERCUTZ

Welcome to the third Tufflips-approved SANJAY AND CRAIG graphic novel from Papercutz—those selfless, selfie-taking, comics-loving, workaholics dedicated to publishing great graphic novels for all ages. I'm Jim Salicrup, Editor-in-Chief and the original Old Kid on the Block, and I'm here to make a really BIG ANNOUNCEMENT…

If you enjoyed this SANJAY AND CRAIG graphic novel, you'll be thrilled to learn that Sanjay and Craig will soon return in the upcoming, all-new NICKELODEON PANDEMONIUM #1 graphic novel. Not only will it feature all-new SANJAY AND CRAIG comics, but it'll feature new comics starring HARVEY BEAKS, PIG GOAT BANANA CRICKET, and BREADWINNERS as well. Like the comics-filled NICKELODEON MAGAZINE, NICKELODEON PANDEMONIUM will be like the comics version of watching Nickelodeon—showcasing multiple Nick stars in every volume!

And let's not forget that Sanjay and Craig will continue to appear in NICKELODEON MAGAZINE, which also includes all sorts of bonus features in every issue. Past issues have included Sanjay and Craig Halloween masks and Sanjay and Craig posters. And of course, Sanjay and Craig continue to appear on Nickelodeon.

While the animated versions of Sanjay and Craig have the added advantage of sound and motion, it's amazing what a great job writer Eric Esquivel and artists Sam Spina, James Kaminski, and others have done, bringing Sanjay and Craig alive in comics form. Their stories started out great, and unbelievably they have just gotten better and better, and funnier and funnier.

I've got to confess, between the TV series and comics, I don't think of Sanjay and Craig as fictitious characters, even though I "know" they really are. To me they're as real as anyone else in my life. And I know many Sanjay and Craig fans feel the exact same way. I'm just lucky to be one of the first people to see their comicbook adventures after editors "Busy" Bethany Bryan and "Judicious" Joan Hilty have put them together!

And speaking of getting a first look at great comics, have we got a special treat for you—we managed to squeeze in a preview of one of the stories from HARVEY BEAKS #2 "It's Crazy Time." The story's "To Dare or Not To Dare," written by Kevin Kramer and illustrated by Brandon B, and Harvey has to face one of his greatest challenges yet! We were able to fit this in as we've added more pages to this third SANJAY AND CRAIG graphic novel, without increasing the price by even a penny (Pepper)! You're welcome!

Jim

STAY IN TOUCH!

EMAIL: salicrup@papercutz.com
WEB: papercutz.com
TWITTER: @papercutzgn
FACEBOOK: PAPERCUTZGRAPHICNOVELS
FANMAIL: Papercutz, 160 Broadway, Suite 700, East Wing, New York, NY 10038

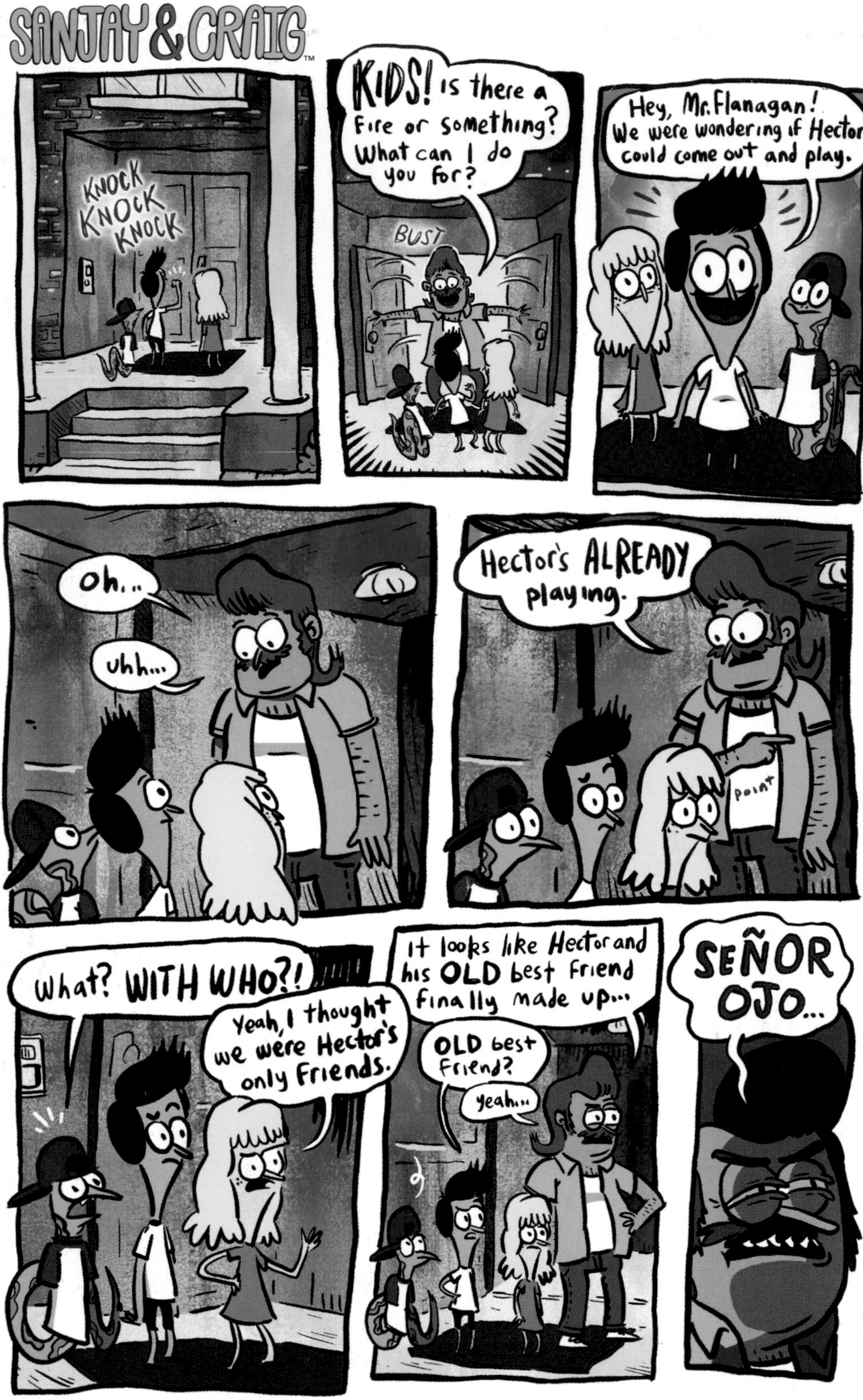

SANJAY & CRAIG
KNOCK KNOCK KNOCK
KIDS! is there a fire or something? What can I do you for?
BUST
Hey, Mr. Flanagan! We were wondering if Hector could come out and play.
Oh...
uhh...
Hector's ALREADY playing.
POINT
What? WITH WHO?!
Yeah, I thought we were Hector's only friends.
It looks like Hector and his OLD best friend finally made up...
OLD best friend?
yeah...
SEÑOR OJO...

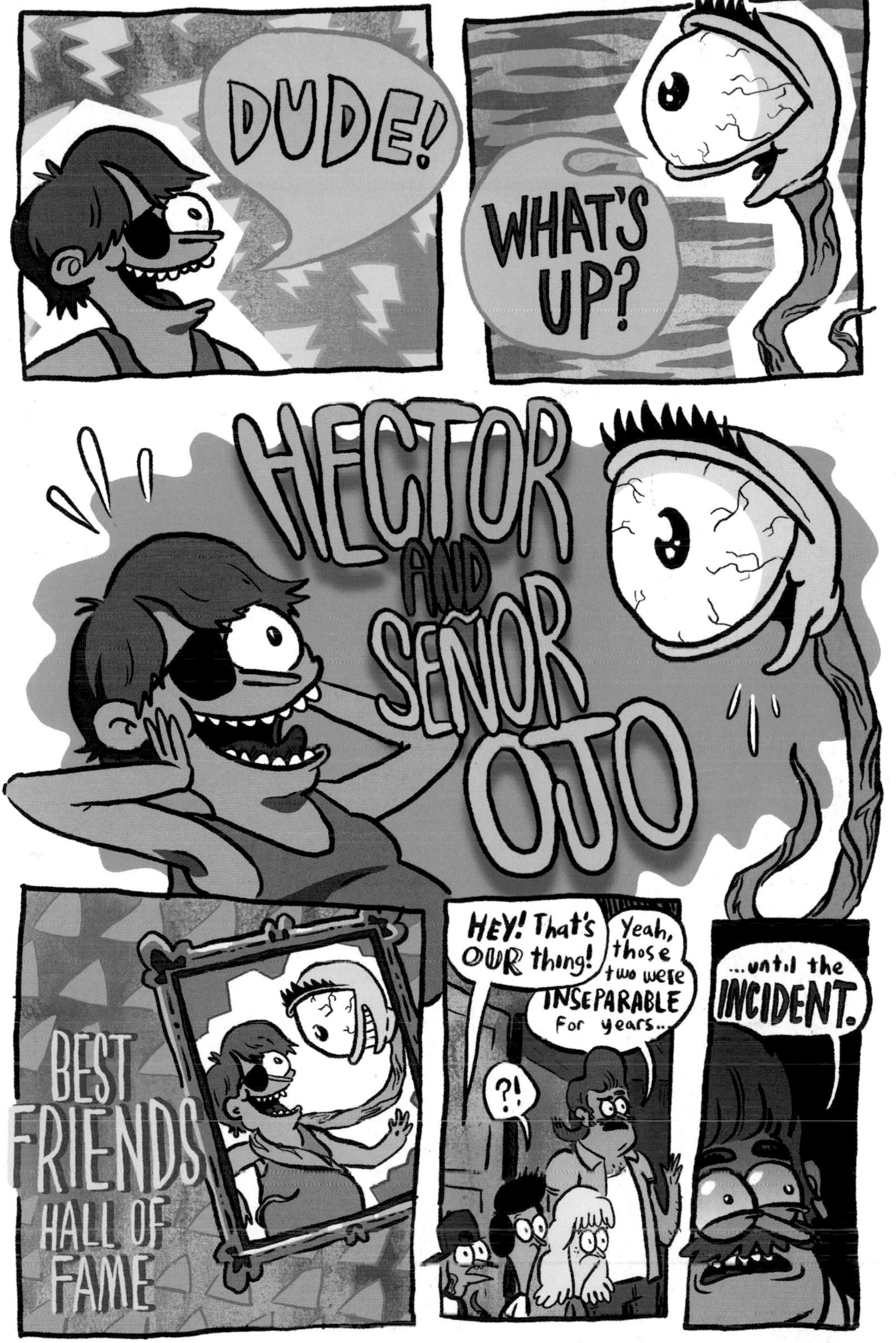
DUDE!
WHAT'S UP?
HECTOR AND SEÑOR OJO
BEST FRIENDS HALL OF FAME
HEY! That's OUR thing!
Yeah, those two were INSEPARABLE For years...
?!
...until the INCIDENT.

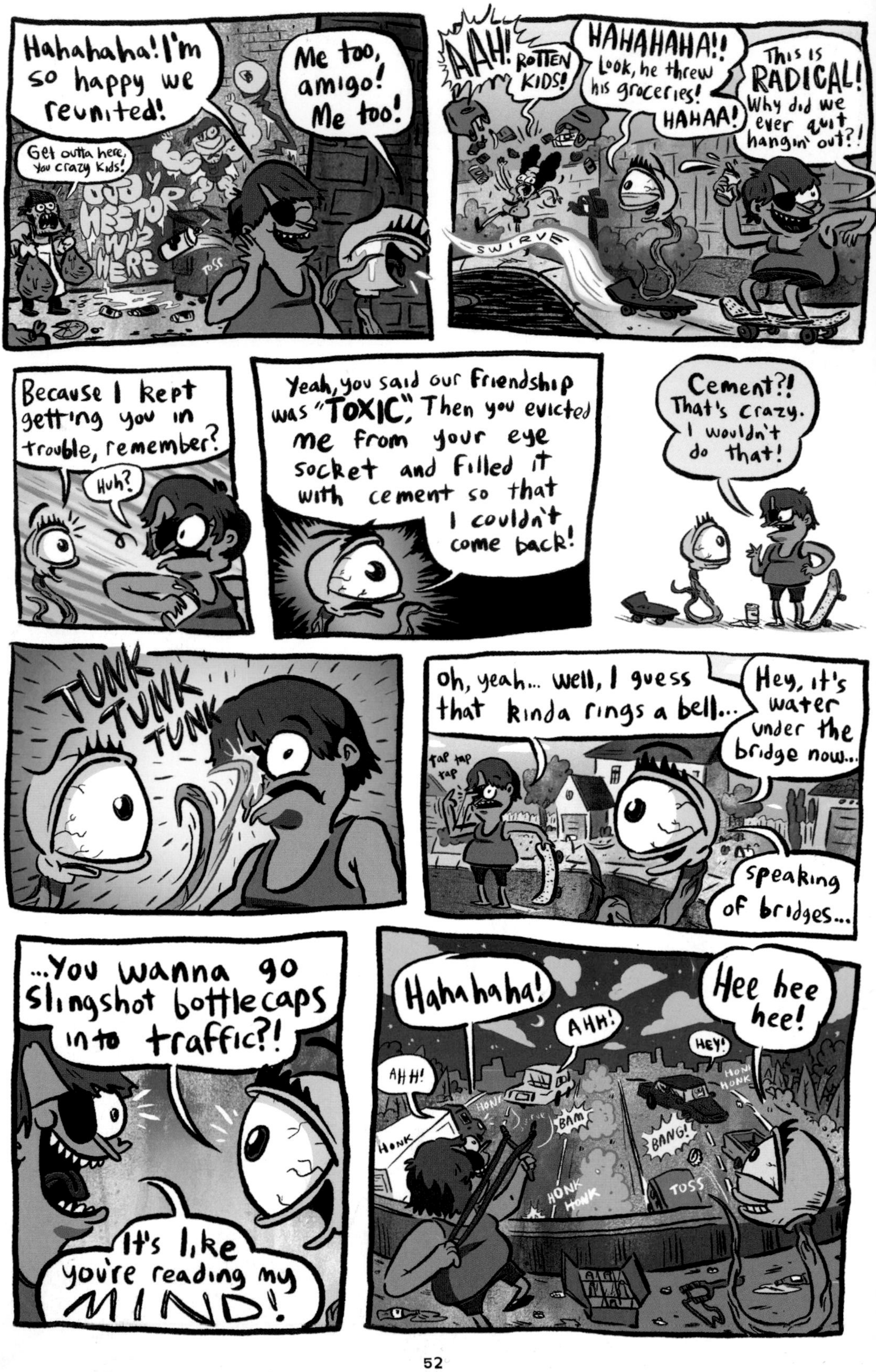

Hahahaha! I'm so happy we reunited!
Me too, amigo! Me too!
Get outta here, you crazy kids!
TOSS
AAH!
ROTTEN KIDS!
HAHAHAHA!! Look, he threw his groceries!
HAHAA!
This is RADICAL! Why did we ever quit hangin' out?!
SWIRVE
Because I kept getting you in trouble, remember?
Huh?
Yeah, you said our friendship was "TOXIC." Then you evicted me from your eye socket and filled it with cement so that I couldn't come back!
Cement?! That's crazy. I wouldn't do that!
TUNK TUNK TUNK
Oh, yeah... well, I guess that kinda rings a bell...
Hey, it's water under the bridge now...
tap tap tap
Speaking of bridges...
...You wanna go slingshot bottlecaps into traffic?!
It's like you're reading my MIND!
Hahahaha!
Hee hee hee!
AHH!
AHH!
HEY!
HONK
BAM
BANG!
HONK HONK
TOSS

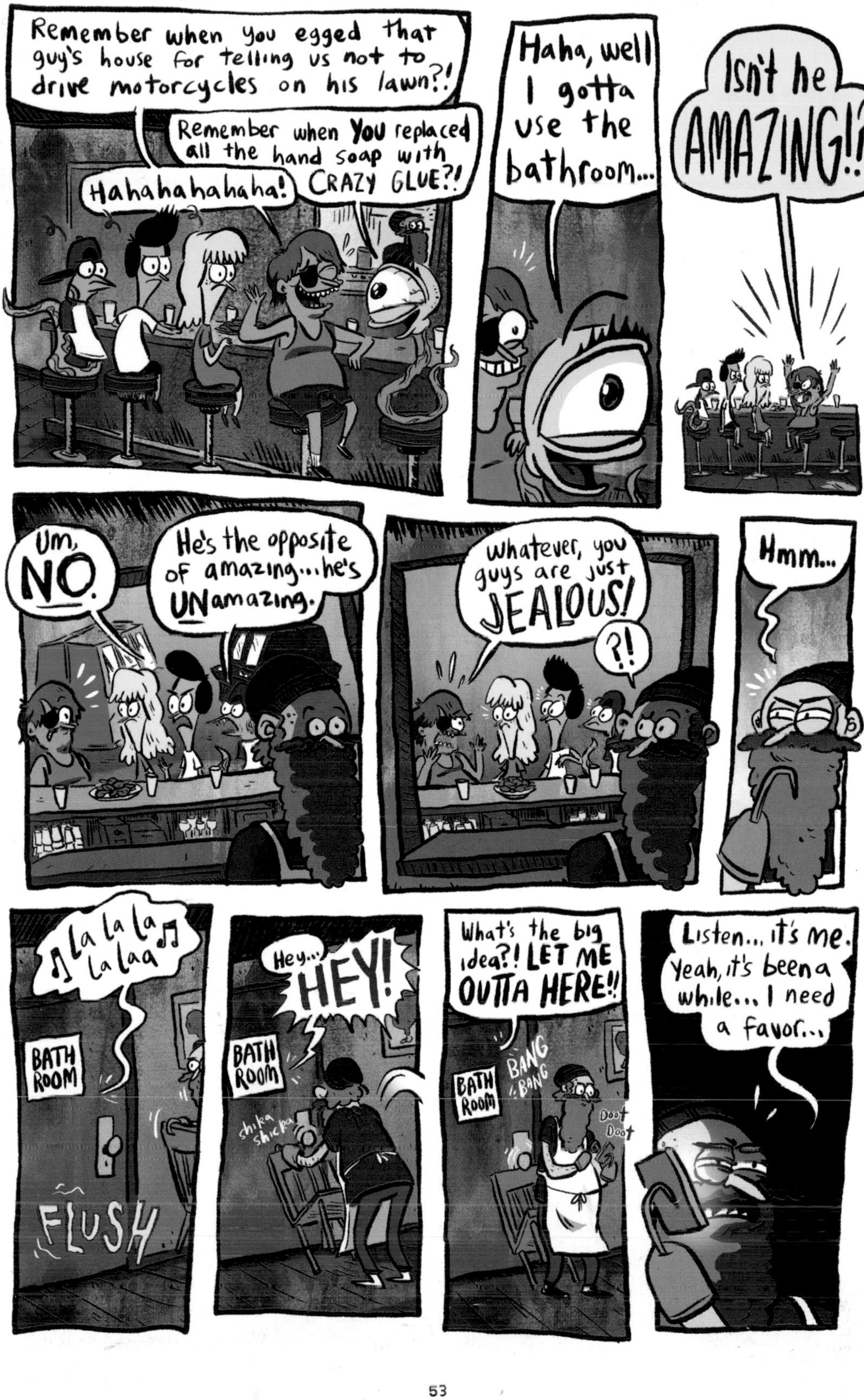
Remember when you egged that guy's house for telling us not to drive motorcycles on his lawn?!
Hahahahahahaha!
Remember when YOU replaced all the hand soap with CRAZY GLUE?!
Haha, well I gotta use the bathroom...
Isn't he AMAZING!?
Um, NO.
He's the opposite of amazing... he's UNamazing.
Whatever, you guys are just JEALOUS!
?!
Hmm...
La la la la laa
BATH ROOM
FLUSH
Hey... HEY!
BATH ROOM
shicka shicka
What's the big idea?! LET ME OUTTA HERE!!
BATH ROOM
BANG BANG
Doot Doot
Listen... it's me. Yeah, it's been a while... I need a favor...

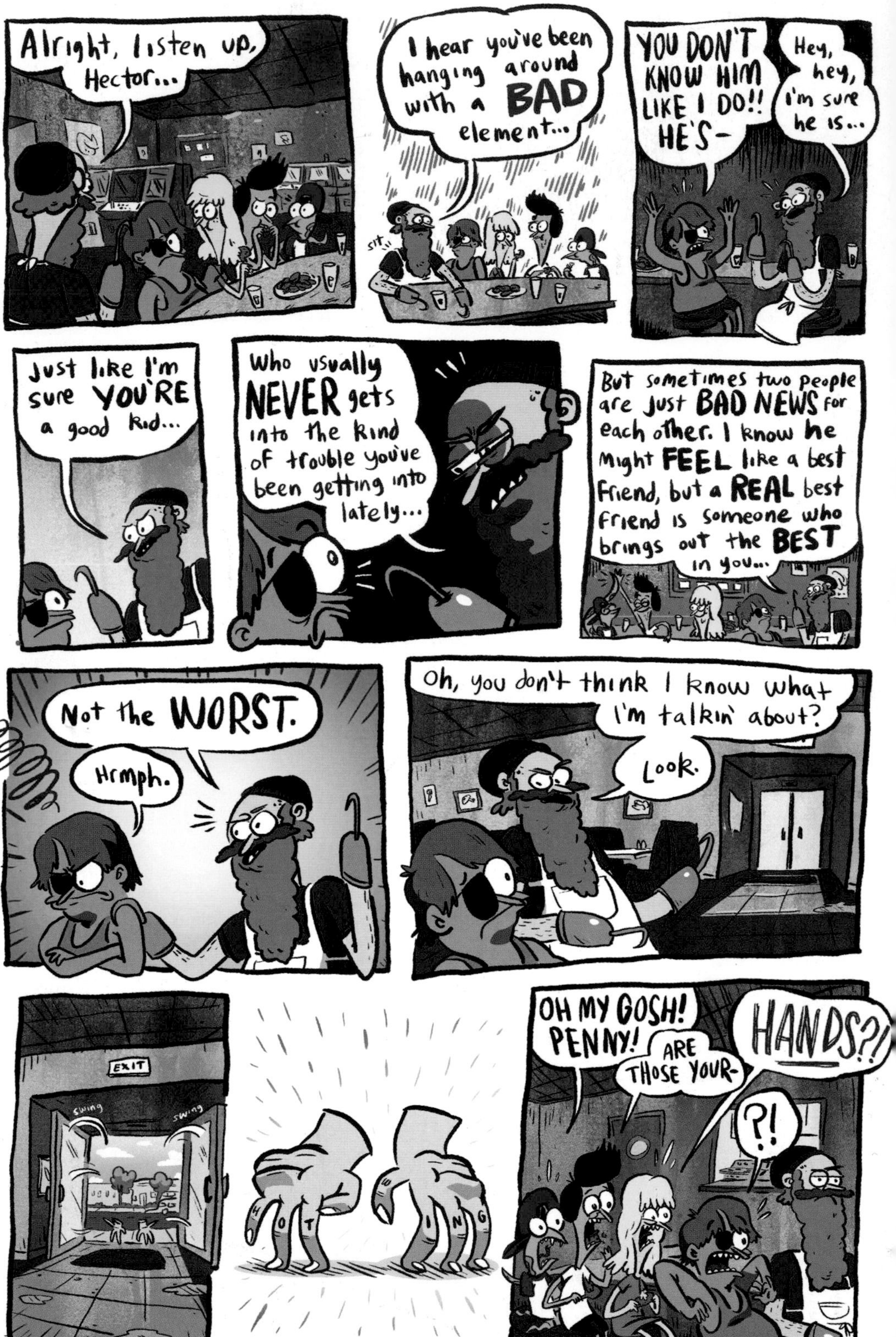
Alright, listen up, Hector...
I hear you've been hanging around with a BAD element...
SIT
YOU DON'T KNOW HIM LIKE I DO!! HE'S-
Hey, hey, I'm sure he is...
Just like I'm sure YOU'RE a good kid...
Who usually NEVER gets into the kind of trouble you've been getting into lately...
But sometimes two people are just BAD NEWS for each other. I know he might FEEL like a best friend, but a REAL best friend is someone who brings out the BEST in you...
Not the WORST.
Hrmph.
Oh, you don't think I know what I'm talkin' about?
Look.
EXIT
swing
swing
OH MY GOSH! PENNY!
ARE THOSE YOUR-
HANDS?!
?!

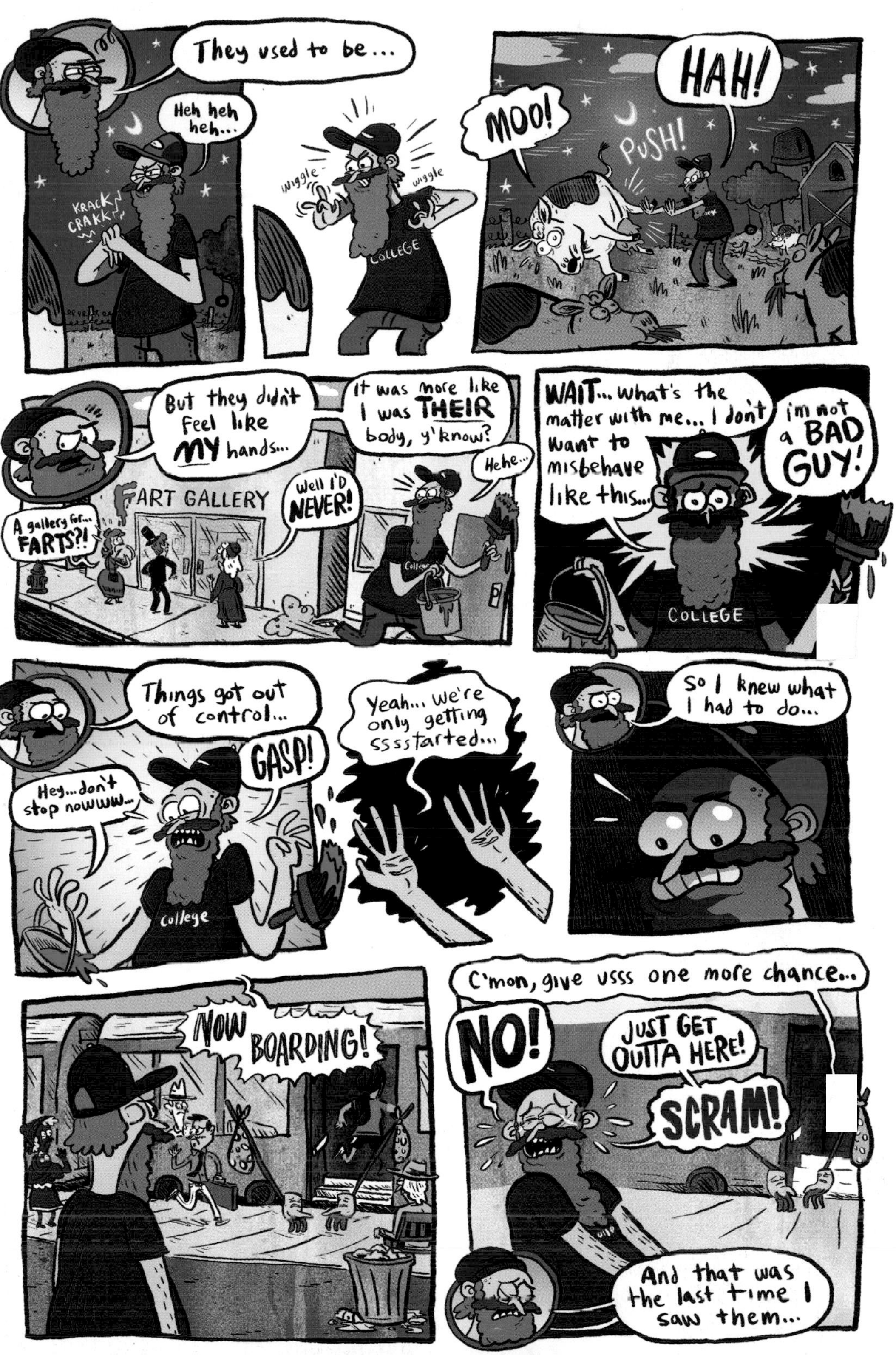
They used to be...
Heh heh heh...
KRACK CRAKK
wiggle
wiggle
COLLEGE
MOO!
HAH!
PUSH!
But they didn't feel like MY hands...
It was more like I was THEIR body, y'know?
FART GALLERY
A gallery for... FARTS?!
Well I'D NEVER!
Hehe...
College
WAIT... what's the matter with me... I don't want to misbehave like this...
i'm not a BAD GUY!
COLLEGE
Things got out of control...
GASP!
Hey...don't stop nowww...
College
Yeah... we're only getting sssstarted...
So I knew what I had to do...
NOW BOARDING!
C'mon, give usss one more chance...
NO!
JUST GET OUTTA HERE!
SCRAM!
And that was the last time I saw them...

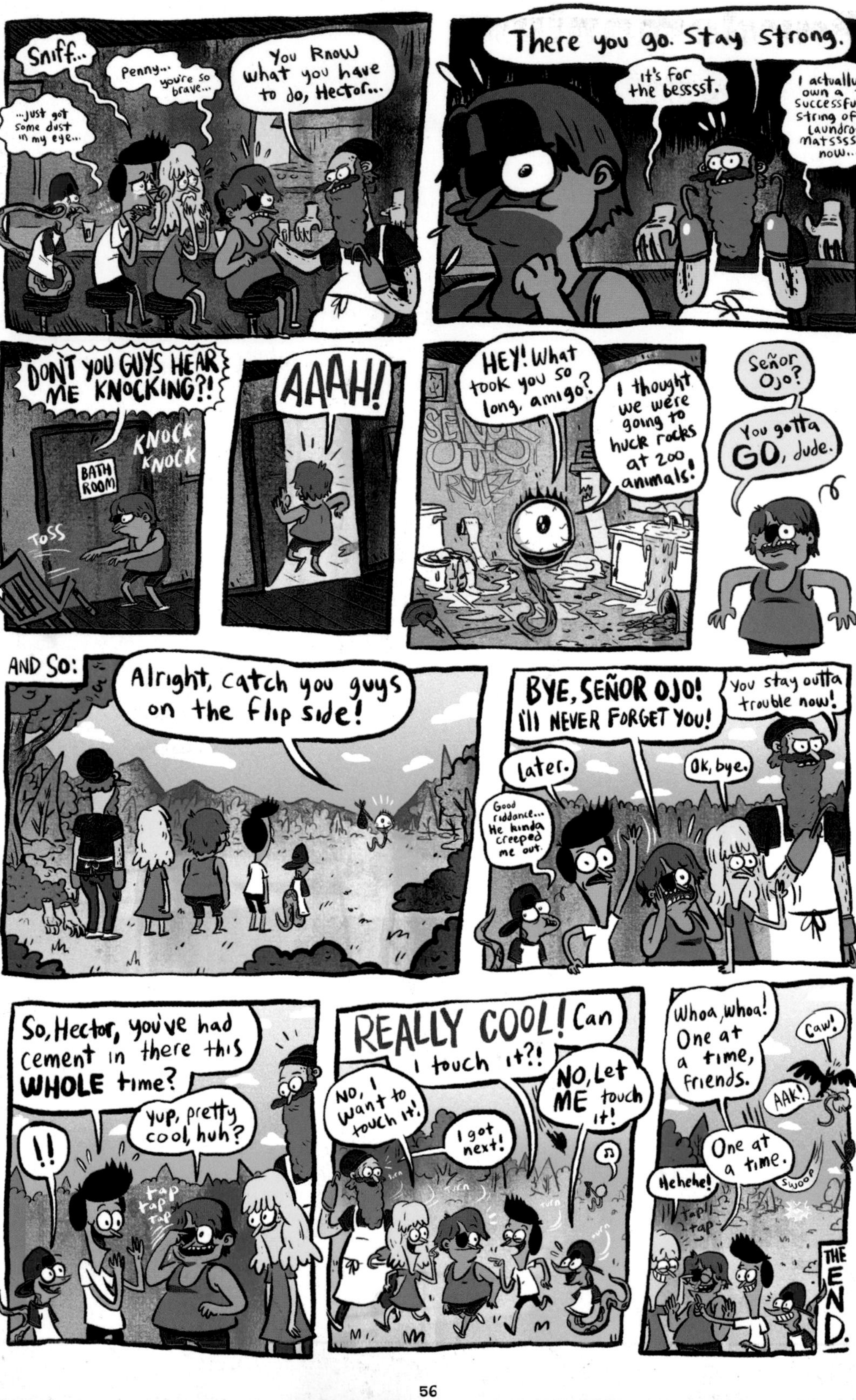
Sniff...
Penny... you're so brave...
You know what you have to do, Hector...
...just got some dust in my eye...
There you go. Stay strong.
It's for the bessssst.
I actually own a successful string of laundromatsssss now...
DON'T YOU GUYS HEAR ME KNOCKING?!
KNOCK KNOCK
BATH ROOM
TOSS
AAAH!
HEY! What took you so long, amigo?
I thought we were going to huck rocks at zoo animals!
Señor Ojo?
You gotta GO, dude.
AND SO:
Alright, catch you guys on the flip side!
BYE, SEÑOR OJO! I'LL NEVER FORGET YOU!
You stay outta trouble now!
Later.
Ok, bye.
Good riddance... He kinda creeped me out.
So, Hector, you've had cement in there this WHOLE time?
!!
Yup, pretty cool, huh?
tap tap tap
REALLY COOL! Can I touch it?!
No, I want to touch it!
I got next!
NO, Let ME touch it!
Whoa, whoa! One at a time, friends.
Caw!
AAK!
One at a time.
Hehehe!
tap tap
SWOOP
THE END.

nickelodeon
PANDEMONIUM!
A COLLECTION OF YOUR FAVORITE TV COMICS
PAPERCUTZ

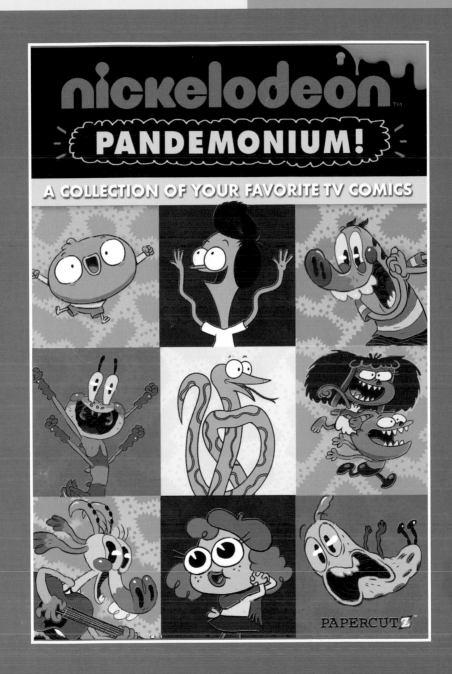

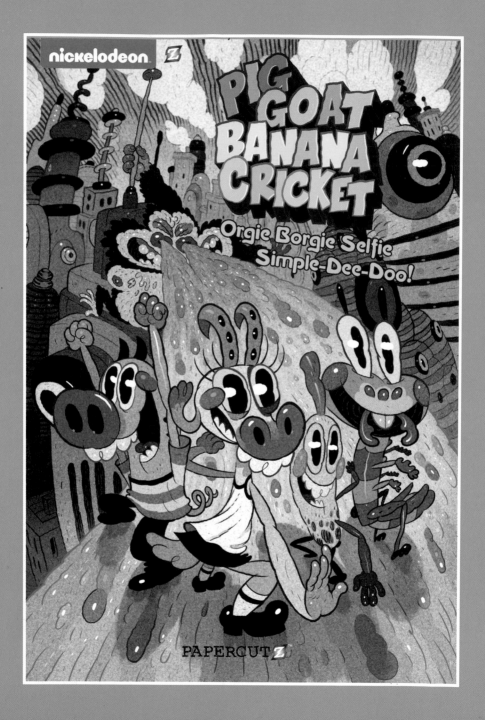

Coming May 2016

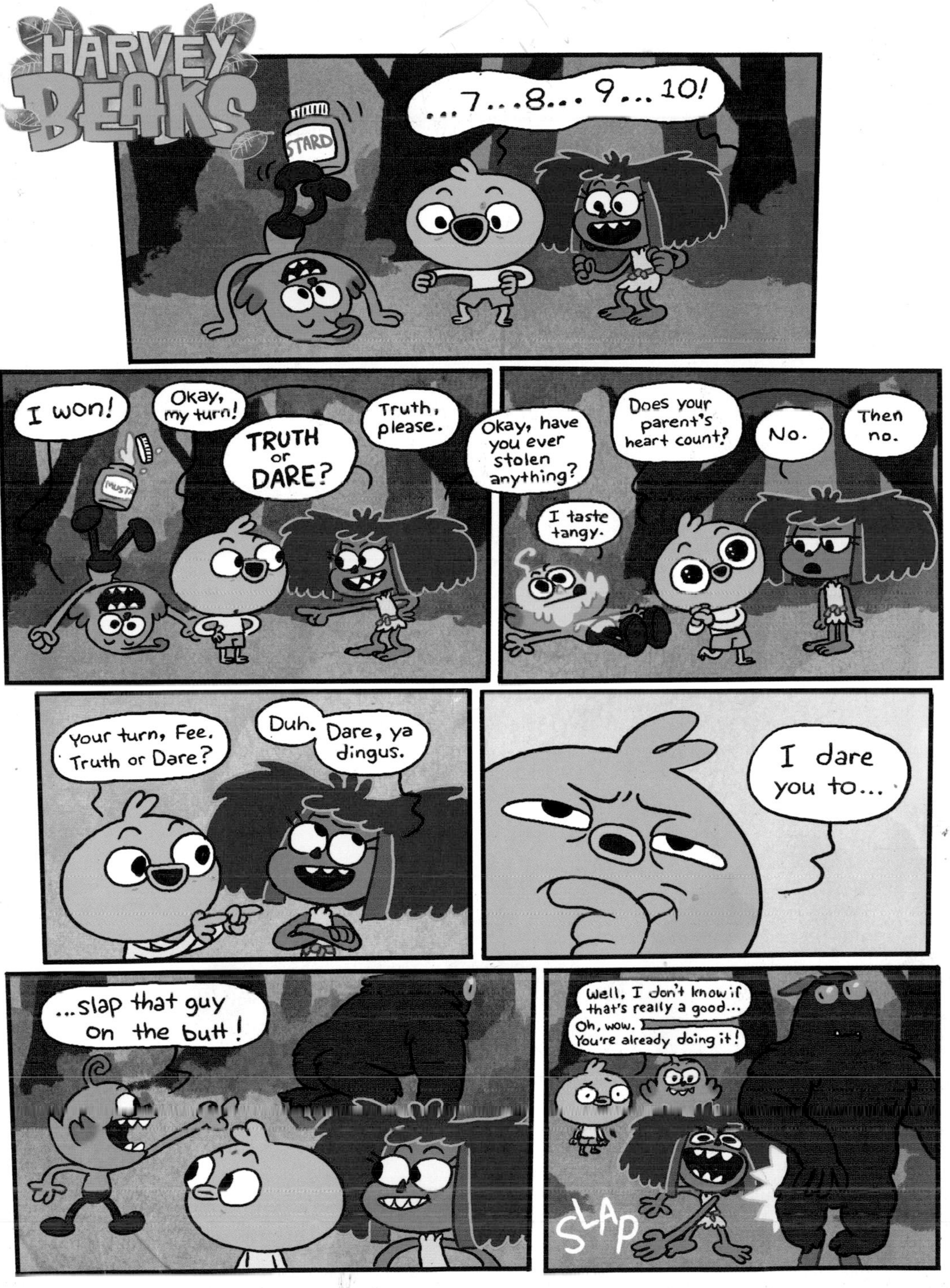
HARVEY BEAKS
STARD
...7...8...9...10!
I won!
Okay, my turn!
TRUTH or DARE?
Truth, please.
Okay, have you ever stolen anything?
I taste tangy.
Does your parent's heart count?
No.
Then no.
Your turn, Fee. Truth or Dare?
Duh.
Dare, ya dingus.
I dare you to...
...slap that guy on the butt!
Well, I don't know if that's really a good...
Oh, wow. You're already doing it!
SLAP

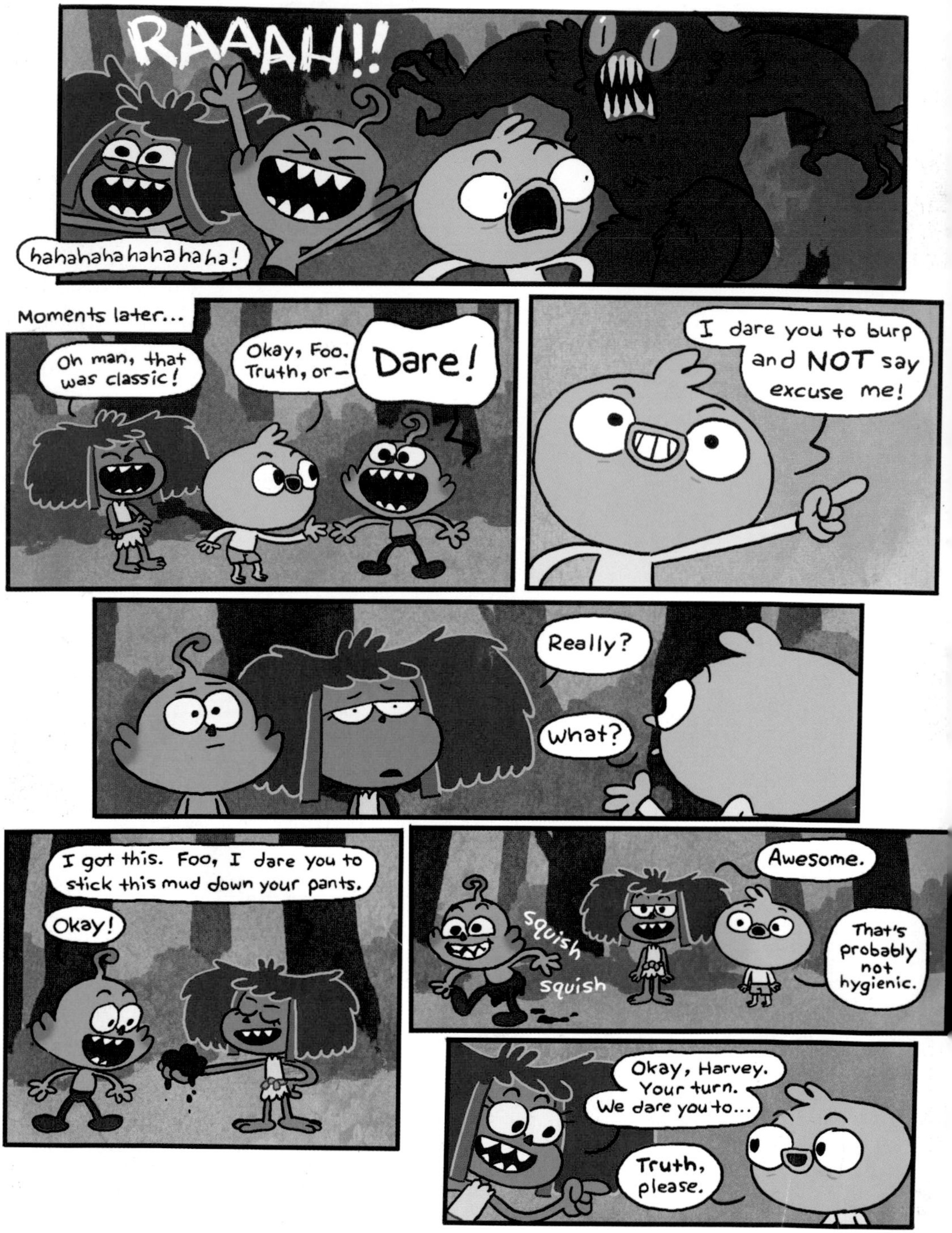
RAAAH!!
hahahahahahahaha!
Moments later...
Oh man, that was classic!
Okay, Foo. Truth, or—
Dare!
I dare you to burp and NOT say excuse me!
Really?
What?
I got this. Foo, I dare you to stick this mud down your pants.
Okay!
Awesome.
squish
squish
That's probably not hygienic.
Okay, Harvey. Your turn. We dare you to...
Truth, please.

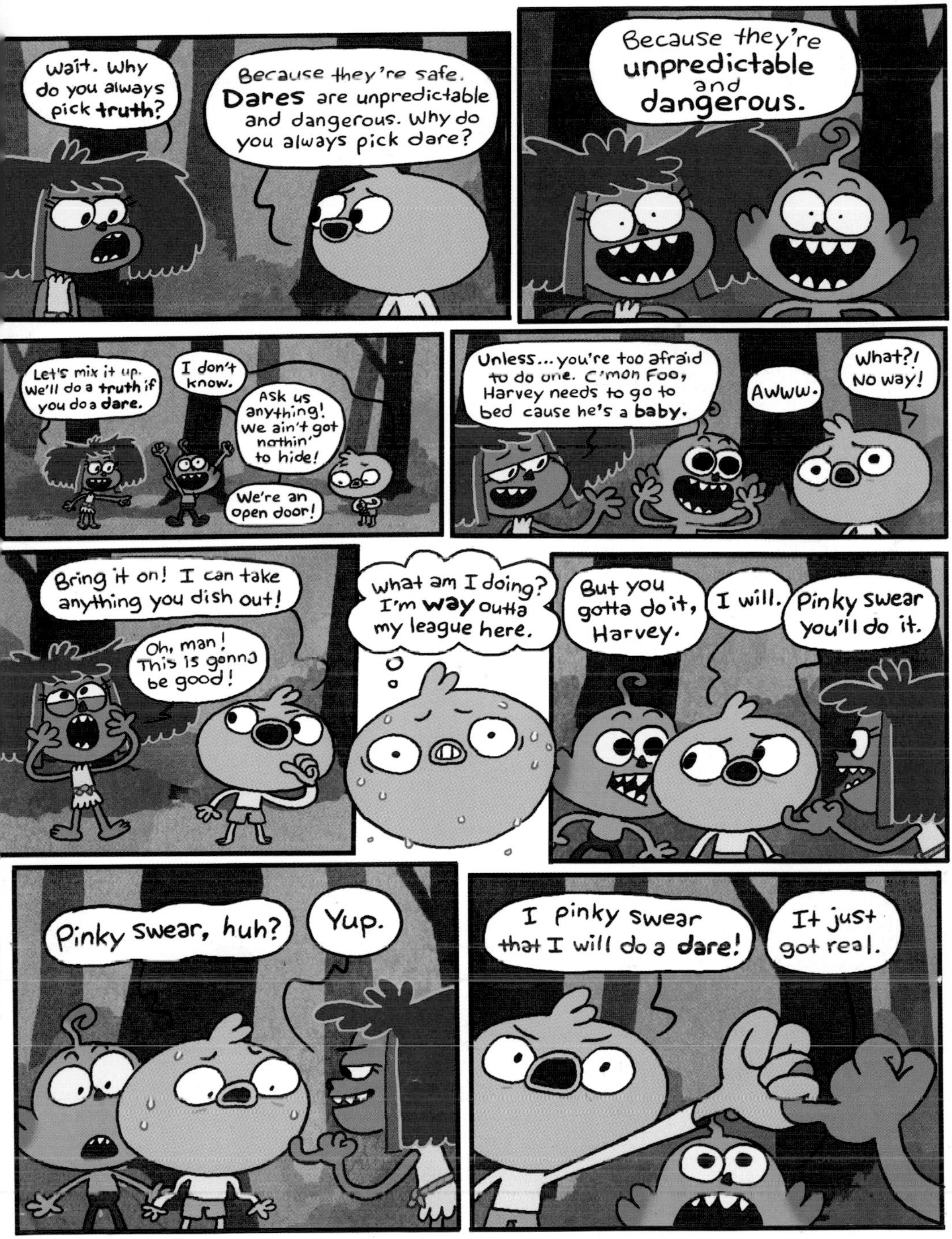
Wait. Why do you always pick truth?
Because they're safe. Dares are unpredictable and dangerous. Why do you always pick dare?
Because they're unpredictable and dangerous.
Let's mix it up. We'll do a truth if you do a dare.
I don't know.
Ask us anything! We ain't got nothin' to hide!
We're an open door!
Unless... you're too afraid to do one. C'mon Foo, Harvey needs to go to bed cause he's a baby.
AWWW.
What?! No way!
Bring it on! I can take anything you dish out!
Oh, man! This is gonna be good!
What am I doing? I'm way outta my league here.
But you gotta do it, Harvey.
I will.
Pinky swear you'll do it.
Pinky swear, huh?
Yup.
I pinky swear that I will do a dare!
It just got real.

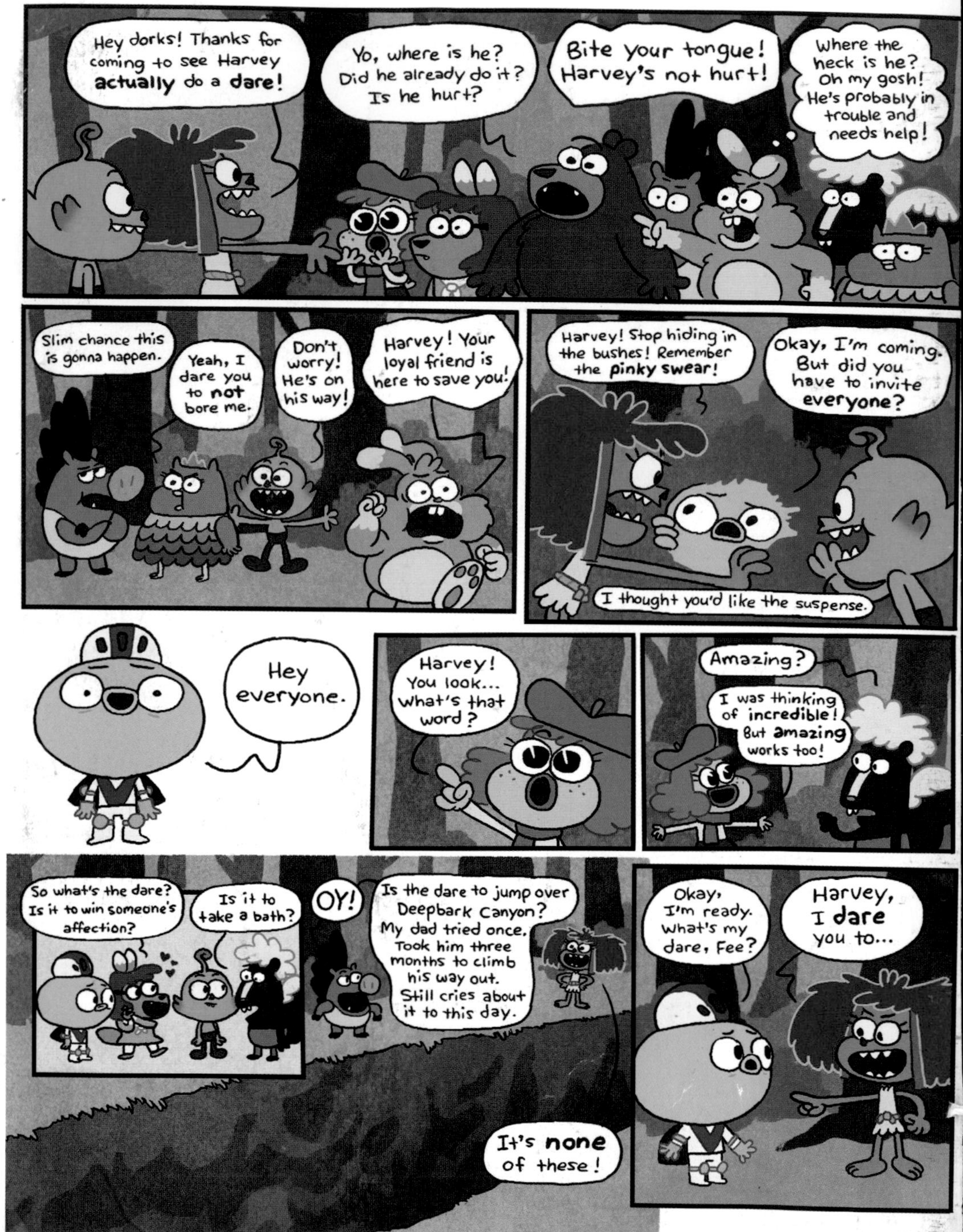
Hey dorks! Thanks for coming to see Harvey **actually** do a **dare**!
Yo, where is he? Did he already do it? Is he hurt?
Bite your tongue! Harvey's not hurt!
Where the heck is he? Oh my gosh! He's probably in trouble and needs help!
Slim chance this is gonna happen.
Yeah, I dare you to **not** bore me.
Don't worry! He's on his way!
Harvey! Your loyal friend is here to save you!
Harvey! Stop hiding in the bushes! Remember the **pinky swear**!
Okay, I'm coming. But did you have to invite **everyone**?
I thought you'd like the suspense.
Hey everyone.
Harvey! You look... what's that word?
Amazing?
I was thinking of **incredible**! But **amazing** works too!
So what's the dare? Is it to win someone's affection?
Is it to take a bath?
OY!
Is the dare to jump over Deepbark Canyon? My dad tried once. Took him three months to climb his way out. Still cries about it to this day.
It's **none** of these!
Okay, I'm ready. What's my dare, Fee?
Harvey, I **dare** you to...

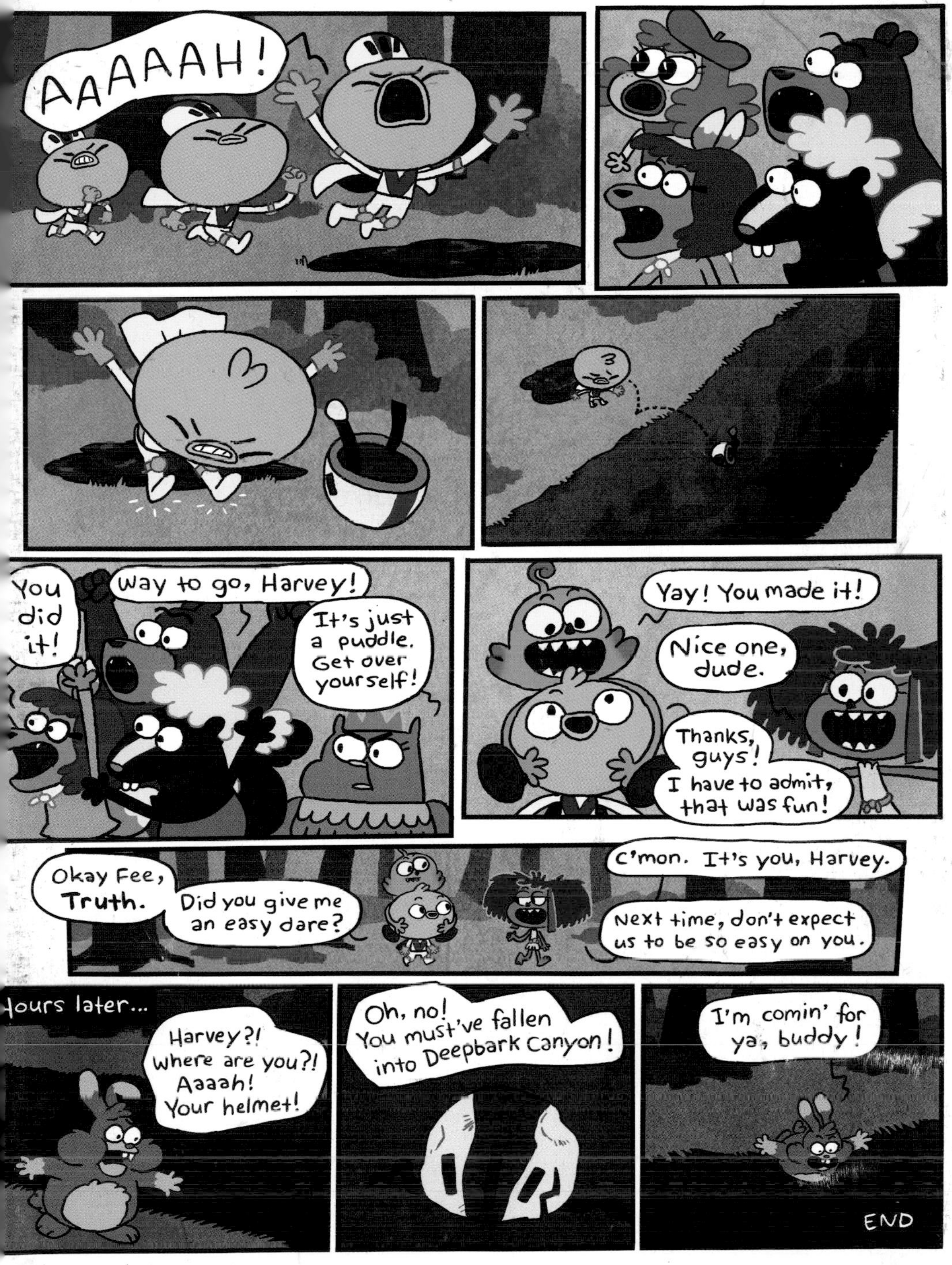

AAAAAH!
You did it!
Way to go, Harvey!
It's just a puddle. Get over yourself!
Yay! You made it!
Nice one, dude.
Thanks, guys! I have to admit, that was fun!
Okay Fee, Truth.
Did you give me an easy dare?
C'mon. It's you, Harvey.
Next time, don't expect us to be so easy on you.
Hours later...
Harvey?! Where are you?! Aaaah! Your helmet!
Oh, no! You must've fallen into Deepbark Canyon!
I'm comin' for ya, buddy!
END

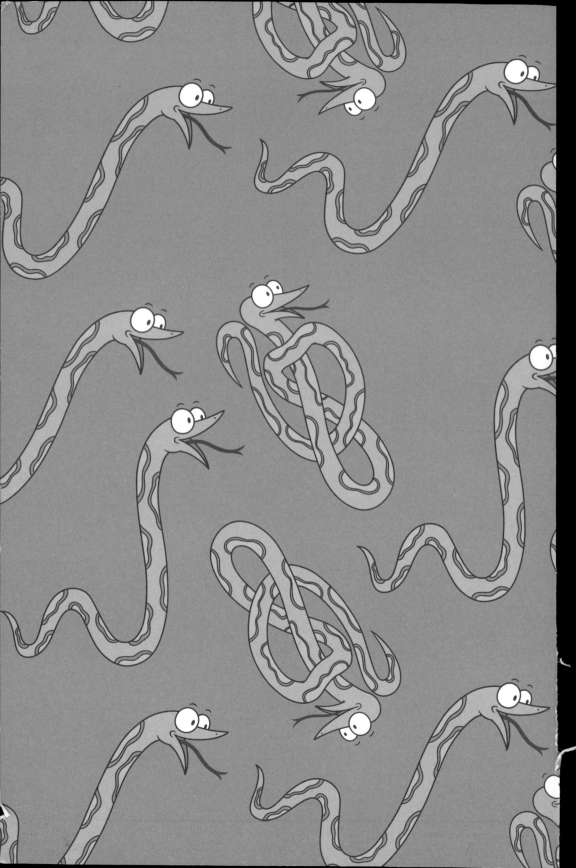